ABOUT THIS BOOK

Welcome to Havenwood Falls, a small town in the majestic mountains of Colorado. A town where legacies began centuries ago, bloodlines run deep, and dark secrets abound. A town where nobody is what you think, where truths pose as lies, and where myths blend with reality. A place where everyone has a story. Including the high schoolers. This is only but one . . .

Eris Blaekthorn can't believe what she and her father find when two strangers come knocking on their door. According to the visitors, a memory spell caused them to forget a place called Havenwood Falls, including their life there and all the people in it. But when the strangers remove the spell, secrets from the past start to unravel.

Eris learns she has an older brother in the small Colorado mountain town. He's trapped in a coma caused by dark magic. But they don't know who did it or how. Her father agrees to leave their home in New Mexico and return to Havenwood Falls—a place he left to keep Eris safe. There, she learns about her family history and who she really is, which becomes the biggest surprise of all.

She also meets Rylan Gilles, a senior at Havenwood Falls High, and her brother's friend. He's beautiful and snarky, and their attraction to each other can't be denied. As events start to spiral and danger rises, Eris turns to Rylan for help in finding the person who spelled her brother so she can save his life.

BOUND BY SHADOWS

A HAVENWOOD FALLS HIGH NOVELLA

CAMEO RENAE

HAVENWOOD FALLS HIGH BOOKS

Written in the Stars by Kallie Ross

Reawakened by Morgan Wylie

The Fall by Kristen Yard

Somewhere Within by Amy Hale

Awaken the Soul by Michele G. Miller

Bound by Shadows by Cameo Renae

Fata Morgana by E.J. Fechenda

Forever Emeline by Katie M. John

Reclamation by AnnaLisa Grant

Avenoir by Daniele Lanzarotta

Avenge the Heart by Michele G. Miller

Curse the Night by R.K. Ryals

Blood & Iron by Amy Hale

Shadows & Spells by Cameo Renae

Falling Deep by J.L. Weil

Saving Infiniti by Rose Garcia

Willful by Liz Ferry

Cast in Moonlight by Ali Winters

Promise the Moon by Kallie Ross

Blurred Lines by Daniele Lanzarotta

Ascending Darkness by J.L. Weil

Finding Infiniti by Rose Garcia

Unicorn's Lament by Megan Linski

Paper Bird by Amy Richie

Predestined by Valia Lind

Rediscovered by Morgan Wylie

Ashes of Fate by Apryl Baker

Stay up to date at www.HavenwoodFalls.com

OTHER BOOKS BY CAMEO RENAE

The Hidden Wings Series (Complete Series)

Hidden Wings

Broken Wings

Tethered Wings

Gilded Wings

Wings of Vengeance

Midway Series (Hidden Wings Spin-Off)

Guarding Eden

Saving Thomas – Coming Soon!

The After Light Saga (Complete Series)

ARV-3

Sanctum

Intransigent

Hostile

Retribution

In My Dreams Duology

In My Dreams

In My Reality

This book is dedicated to all those who embrace their weirdness.
Keep life interesting and entertaining.
Keep it real.

CHAPTER 1

*C*hange was coming. I not only knew it—I felt it. Not just because New Year's was a few days away, but because of the newly gained sense I'd acquired when I turned sixteen a little over a year ago. So I wasn't hugely surprised when the doorbell rang in our quiet neighborhood on an uneventful Saturday night.

"I'll get it," I said, placing the last clean dinner plate in the dish drain, then wiping my hands dry on a dish towel.

My dad's watchful eyes were on me as I strode for the door. He was overprotective, and although I felt suffocated at times, I understood. It'd been just the two of us for as long as I could remember.

My father had chosen our neighborhood in New Mexico because it was safe and filled with dozens of cautious, watchful eyes. Especially the pair that belonged to the old lady across the street who moved in a few weeks after we did. She used to babysit me when I was younger, but not since I turned sixteen and pleaded with my dad that I was old enough to watch myself.

Old Ms. Gingrich—the Grinch—was a stiff and nosey woman who smelled of mothballs and strong herbs. She was strict and watched me like a hawk.

I wouldn't have been surprised if she was the one who rang the doorbell, hunched over, her wiry white hair in a tight bun, with some odd request for my dad. It happened so often, I wondered if she was going senile and thought he was her son.

As I reached the door and pulled it open, it wasn't the Grinch who greeted me, but two unfamiliar faces.

The first was a pretty woman with pale skin and short brown hair. The man standing next to her was tall with broad shoulders, dark brown hair, and chocolate eyes specked with gold.

"Can I help you?" I asked.

"Eris?" His eyes widened like he knew me. As he stepped forward, I stepped back.

He knew my name. How?

His strong scent wafted to my nose, woodsy and musky. A powerful smell for a powerful-looking man. I couldn't help but stare at him. There was something oddly familiar I couldn't put my finger on. The woman, I was sure I'd never seen before.

Footsteps pounded behind me. "I'm sorry, but we don't accept solicitors here," my dad said firmly.

The man's eyes moved to my dad, still filled with recognition. "Piers?"

My father stepped in front of me, pushing me behind him—a defensive move. Then, he went quiet as he took in the man's face.

"Garrick?" His expression twisted.

"It's been too long," the man replied.

The two of them collided in a hug, and I stood there feeling a mixture of surprise and confusion. My dad never hugged anyone like that, with so much emotion and intensity.

"Where the hell have you been?" my dad asked, grabbing the man's shoulders. "All this time, I—I thought you were dead."

"Dad?" I asked, trying to make sense of what was going on.

"It's okay, Eris," he said, turning toward me. "This is your long-lost uncle Garrick."

"Wait. What?" I gasped. "I have an uncle?"

"Actually, you have two," Garrick replied. "But I'm the handsome one." He winked, then laughed, turning his attention back to my father.

"Dad, why didn't you tell me?" I never knew I had other living family members.

My dad shook his head. "I'm sorry, Eris. There is so much I just can't remember."

"Piers, I know this is a huge surprise, and believe me, I understand." He turned to the woman. "This is Lyra Beaumont. We're here because—well—it's a bit complicated." He looked at the woman and ran a hand through his thick, dark hair. He was having trouble explaining their reasons for being here, frustration written all over his face. "We've come with bad news of a close family member."

"Is it Barney? Is he okay?" My dad's face went pale.

I assumed Barney was the "not as handsome" uncle.

Garrick shook his head. "No. Barney's fine. We're here about your son, Piers."

My father's eyes narrowed, then he glanced back at me, his expression unreadable. I shook my head and looked back at the man claiming to be my uncle. I didn't have a brother. That was the kind of thing someone didn't forget.

"Garrick, I don't have a son," my dad replied.

Garrick slowly reached into his pocket and pulled out a paper, then offered it to my dad.

Tiptoeing, I peeked over his shoulder to see an old photograph that had been folded in half, but I immediately recognized three of the faces. My dad, my mom, and me. But I was much younger. And there was someone standing next to me . . . a boy with his arm over my shoulder. I could see the resemblance. He had the same golden-brown hair and the same shaped eyes as me, only he was a foot taller and looked a few years older.

"You have a son, Piers, and if you let us in, I'll explain why you don't remember him."

My father paused, looking at the picture. I could see the tension in his jaw. "How did you get this?" my dad snapped, holding the picture up. "Is this a fake?"

Garrick held up both hands in front of him. "It's real. I assure you."

"Why, after all this time, would you show up and tell me about a son I don't have?" A deep guttural growl erupted from my dad's chest. "What the hell is going on?"

"Piers, I promise we'll explain," Garrick pleaded, turning to Lyra and giving her a nod.

Lyra quickly waved her hand in front of my dad and whispered a single word. I couldn't hear the word, but after she spoke it, my dad took a shaky step back. He shook his head, his eyes blinking rapidly several times.

Then, it was as if a switch had been flipped. His entire demeanor shifted, and his harsh expression was replaced with what I could only describe as understanding.

Could it have been magic?

I was no stranger to magic. Ever since we moved into this house, I could do things no normal kids could do. Like move things with my mind. My first real encounter was when Dad and I were sitting at the dining table eating breakfast. I was tired, and he'd asked me to pass the syrup. In my mind, I willed the syrup to move, and to mine and my dad's surprise, it did. He was not only shocked but immediately concerned and warned me —repetitively—to never, ever use my magic in front of anyone else.

And that wasn't all. Once in a while, whenever I felt really sad or frightened, a glimmer would appear—a small, bright ball of light, about three inches around, and when it came close, it radiated warmth. At first, I was afraid of it, but every time it appeared, it made me feel a lot better. Less . . . alone. I also learned that no one else could see it. So it had become my secret. A glimmer of hope and light that would come whenever the world around me felt dark.

My dad stepped aside, allowing my uncle and the woman into our living room.

"What's the news you came with?" Dad questioned, his arms crossing over his chest. I could see the muscles in his biceps tighten. He was ready to defend us, if he had to.

"I will tell you, but first, Lyra needs to perform a simple ceremony to reverse a memory spell that has been placed on both of you. Once she finishes, it will be much easier to explain."

"Memory spell? What the hell is that?" My father's arms lowered, and a growl rumbled deep in his chest. Garrick stepped back with his hands up in surrender.

"Piers, you know me. You've known me your entire life, and *you* agreed to this spell when you left Havenwood Falls, knowing full well what the repercussions would be."

"Havenwood Falls?" My dad shook his head.

"Yes. Think about it." Garrick approached my dad slowly, carefully. "There is a large chunk of your life missing. That chunk were the years you lived in Havenwood Falls with Aurora and your children. When you left, a memory spell—which is automatically placed on everyone who leaves the town—caused you to forget."

My dad shook his head. "I don't understand what you're saying, but I swear . . . if you do anything that will harm my daughter—"

"I know," Garrick said, his hands still raised. "You just have to trust me, Piers. Let Lyra do her thing, and we can talk after."

"Please, take a seat," the woman said, gesturing to our brown leather couch. She wasn't wasting any time, but I didn't sense any negative vibe from her. That was one thing I could pick up on in most people—if they had good or bad intentions—and my intuition was usually right. I guess my dad didn't feel anything negative either, because he gave me a nod and took a seat on the couch.

Lyra stood in front of us while Garrick paced slowly behind her. "I need you both to relax, close your eyes, and try to clear your mind," she said.

Right. Easier said than done with the gazillion unanswered questions they'd just thrown on us. And the fact I'd just learned I had relatives. Living relatives.

I leaned over to my dad. "Do you trust them?"

His eyes found mine. "I do. I have a feeling they're here to help and not harm."

I nodded, then leaned back. My dad took my hand, which helped me relax a bit.

"Wait a minute," I blurted, my eyes popping back open, finding Lyra. "Is this safe? Our minds won't be scrambled or altered in any way, right?"

Lyra grinned. "It's perfectly safe, dear. I promise there won't be any scrambled minds. I'm just removing a spell. That's it."

"Okay." I sighed loudly, wondering what kind of memories were hidden from me for who knows how long. "Let's do this."

As I closed my eyes, the woman began to chant. As she continued, I focused on the words, relaxed into them, and soon felt a gentle buzz in the air. My head felt tingly and light, like a weight was being lifted. Then, after a few moments, she stopped.

I opened my eyes and found her walking back toward Garrick.

"Is it done?" he whispered.

"Yes, the spell has been removed," she spoke softly. "It might take a while, but they should start to remember things soon."

"Thank you," Garrick replied with a nod.

"Wait," I blurted. "The memory spell—what exactly is it used for and why?"

Garrick sat on the loveseat across from us, his hands folded in front of him. "When you and your dad left Havenwood Falls, the memories of the place, the people in it, and everything that happened there were suppressed. Think of it as a type of amnesia caused by the spell. For me to explain why I've come, we needed to remove that spell. Lyra," his eyes traveled to the woman, "is a witch from Havenwood Falls, and one of the few trusted to reverse it." His eyes darted back and forth between my dad and me, watching us with great anticipation. Then, he clapped his hands together loudly. "So . . . is it working?"

My dad exhaled, pressing his face into his palms.

I was surprised he wasn't saying anything. He normally questioned everything. Why was he so quiet?

He finally sat forward and looked at Garrick. "Right now, all I have is a massive headache." He stood from the couch and began to walk toward the kitchen.

"Where are you going?" I called after him.

"To take something for this throbbing pain in my head."

"Just give the spell some time," Lyra said after him. "You've been gone for quite a while. It might take a bit to unravel all the memories. It's different for everyone."

My father returned a few moments later and plopped down next to me, his elbows pressed against his knees, the picture in his hands. His eyes were narrowed, studying the faces.

We all watched him in silence.

"I've had this emptiness inside I couldn't explain. A hole of sadness I could never fill," he murmured. "Now I understand where it came from. It was the place the memories once were. Memories of them." His finger traced over my mom and the boy in the picture. Then, he quickly swiped a stray tear that escaped his eye and trickled down his cheek.

I'd never seen my dad so shaken, so . . . emotional. He was strong, physically and emotionally, and not once had I ever seen him cry.

"I'm sorry, Piers. What Lyra just did will reverse the spell and return what was hidden these past seven years," Garrick explained, his brow furrowed.

My dad nodded, then closed his eyes. His head fell back onto the couch.

I waited again, for some lightbulb to click on in my mind and all my memories to flood back. But there was nothing. As time ticked on, doubt and frustration set in.

Just before I was about to say something, my dad's head snapped forward, and his eyes went wide, blinking away an invisible fog. He stood from the couch and stared at the man standing in front of him. I saw something in his eyes. Something I couldn't explain.

"You okay?" Garrick asked.

My dad nodded. "I remember."

CHAPTER 2

*G*arrick stood and hugged my dad. "It's great to have you back, brother."

Brother. As they stood together I could see how strong the resemblance was. They had the same features, the same dark hair and gold specks in their dark eyes.

But what about my brother?

"Dad," I spoke, and they went quiet. "Is it true I have a brother?"

His eyes met mine, and there was a short pause before he answered. "Yes, Eris. It's true."

My chest constricted and ached to the point of bursting. He'd forgotten about his son. His *son*. And not only his son . . . *my brother*. How could he allow himself—allow *us*—to forget something so important?

"Why did we forget him?"

"Eris," Garrick cut in, but my mind and the room were spinning. "It was necessary—"

"No!" I yelled, fisting my hands so tightly, my nails cut into my palms. "This is kind of a big deal. Why would anyone want to make me forget that I have a brother? For the past *seven* years I never knew he existed." I could barely breathe, my body shaking as I looked at my dad. "Why did we leave him?"

"Your brother refused to leave Havenwood Falls, and the entire family agreed. We had his best interests at heart," Garrick answered again.

"His best interests?" I snapped, my eyes glaring at him. "How old was he when we left?"

"We recently celebrated his nineteenth birthday."

Nineteen? I quickly did the math, my eyes narrowing on my dad. "You left him when he was twelve? You let *him* make the decision to stay and were okay with it?"

"You don't understand, Eris," Garrick added. "Your brother was troubled at the time, and despite it seeming like an irrational move, we all knew it was the right decision. He's had a good life. I assure you. It just wasn't safe for him to leave with you, and you'll understand why soon."

I couldn't speak, my body shaking. I felt violated. They'd taken something away from me, and I'd had no say in it.

"What's his name?" I didn't want to wait for the damn memories to return to find out.

"Camden," my dad answered. "His name is Camden."

Hot tears filled my eyes and spilled down my cheeks. *Camden.*

"Eris," Lyra spoke softly. "The memory spell is not specific to any individual. Every person, whether a resident or visitor of Havenwood Falls, will not remember the place or anything that happened there once they leave. It's a safeguard."

"A safeguard? For what?"

"Havenwood Falls and many of its residents are *special* and need to be protected," Lyra replied, glancing at Garrick. He nodded in affirmation.

I sighed, claiming defeat. They weren't going to tell me anything else.

"Piers," Garrick said, placing his hands on my dad's shoulders. "The reason we came is because Camden is injured."

"How? What happened?" My father's voice was strained.

"We don't know. He's in a coma, and we believe it's tied to a spell.

Some kind of dark magic. The mages are working on it, but as of now, he's unresponsive."

Mages. Dark magic. A memory spell to make us forget the place. *Special?* Just from those few words alone, I knew Havenwood Falls wasn't a normal community.

"Do you have any idea who did it?" my dad asked.

"No. But the sheriff is investigating. Hopefully we'll have something or someone soon."

I was still in shock and disbelief. I wanted answers—firm answers I could grasp on to—and the only one to give them to me was . . .

"Dad? What happened in Havenwood Falls that made us leave?"

My dad walked up and put his arm around me, then sat me back down on the couch. "Havenwood Falls was a place we lived with your mother and brother. It's the place you were born, Eris. But something horrible happened. Something I couldn't stop." Tears welled in his eyes, and I could tell he struggled with telling me everything. Telling me the truth. "Soon, I will be able to explain it all to you, but not right now. All you need to know is there were things that happened in Havenwood Falls that forced me to leave and take you with me. Promises I made to your mother. And of course, things I wanted to forget." His head lowered. I could tell that most of his memories had returned. But mine still hadn't. *Why?*

My dad had kept one single picture of my mother, which was framed and placed on our living room mantel. It had been the only evidence I possessed that proved she existed. So many nights I stared at that picture, memorizing the lines of her face. She was beautiful and had so much life in her golden-brown eyes. She was laughing, the sun beaming just as bright as her smile, her golden hair shimmering. When I closed my eyes, I could almost see her and often imagined what it would have been like to have her in my life. How different it would have been.

My dad told me she'd died giving birth to me. He'd handwritten it on the back of the picture.

Aurora Witheridge-Blaekthorn – Beloved wife

Died giving birth to daughter.

But that wasn't true. In the picture Garrick brought, she was there, and I was about nine or ten.

I jumped up to grab her picture from the mantel when my dad pulled Garrick to the side. He tried to talk softly, but I could hear him clearly.

"I'll need to make arrangements for Eris before I leave."

I turned, aghast. "Arrangements? No, Dad. You are *not* leaving me here."

"Eris," my dad exhaled. "There are things in Havenwood Falls that can—"

"Hurt me?" I huffed. "Dad, the world is filled with things that can hurt me. I'm not a child anymore. I'm seventeen. And, besides, you've taught me how to defend myself." He knew that was true. "Dad, please. You can't leave me here. You can't keep me from seeing my brother."

I turned to Garrick and hoped he would help plead my case. "I think she should come, Piers. She might be able to help."

"No. Absolutely not!" my father growled. "I don't want her involved in any of the family issues."

"Piers, you can't keep her away forever. It's in her blood."

"What's in my blood? What aren't you telling me?" I demanded.

"I said no," my dad snarled and walked away. "Besides, she has school work."

"Dad, it's winter break and besides . . . I'm homeschooled," I rebutted.

He wasn't going to budge, so I had to come up with something else. If anyone could change his mind, it was me. I knew him best, and I knew what it took to play his heartstrings. If I could get him thinking, then maybe, I'd have a chance.

I followed him into the kitchen. "Listen, Dad. You have a son in a coma. I agree, you need to go and be with him, but you'll be leaving me here for days, maybe longer, under the supervision of an old woman. What if something happened? You wouldn't be here to protect me. Besides that, I just found out I have a brother who is in a coma. I *need* to be there, too."

Garrick joined us, leaning against the kitchen entryway. "She'll be safe with the family, Piers."

I twirled back, and Garrick winked at me. At that moment, I liked him. I had an uncle who was on my side, and it felt good.

Lyra also stepped in and added, "We can put wards up around your property. She'll be safe as long as she stays within the boundary. Besides, I agree with Garrick. It's better for her to be surrounded by family, and I think it's time—" She stopped.

"Time for what?" I asked. My dad's eyes narrowed.

"To meet your family." She smiled.

I knew that wasn't what she had been about to say, but I took it, because they were pushing for me to go.

My father had taught me everything I needed to know about self-defense and how to use weapons, but there was something about me he didn't know. A secret I'd kept from him, different from the magic I had when I was younger.

Ever since I'd turned sixteen, strange things started happening to me. Things I couldn't explain.

My sense of smell, taste, and hearing were heightened, and I could see extremely well in the dark. Not only that, I felt strong—*really* strong—and could move heavy things with no problem. At first, it terrified me, but I knew that if I told my dad, he'd freak.

He was the kind of dad who would rush to the drugstore and buy a ton of medicine if he heard me cough.

The thing was, since the changes started a year ago, I never got sick. Not once. So, I kept the changes to myself. Besides, I didn't want anyone else to know. They wouldn't understand. I'd read enough books and watched enough movies to know what would happen if I went to a doctor. I'd be tested—poked and prodded—and then they'd give the ultimate answer: "I'm sorry, Mr. Blaekthorn. We don't know what's wrong with her." Then there'd be more experiments, only to get more unanswered results. Nope. I wasn't a damn lab rat.

So, I embraced my oddities.

I knew, deep inside, nothing was wrong with me. Actually, I felt like everything was right.

With the new changes, I was also having a recurring dream of a woman, tall and beautiful, with long golden hair and honey-colored eyes. And with her, always at her side, was a beautiful golden-haired wolf. She would kneel and embrace it, pet its thick fur, and sing sweetly to it, lulling the wolf to sleep. When her eyes found mine again, she would smile, and the dream would end.

I had no idea what the dream meant, but I always felt so peaceful when I would wake after it. It happened so often, I felt like I knew the woman. She looked a lot like my mother, but she wasn't her. She was older, and I often wondered if she was my estranged grandmother. The woman I was told left after my grandfather died, without a word.

Another knock on the door made me stiffen. This time, my dad went to get it.

"Ms. Gingrich," he said, and I sighed.

"Is everything all right?" she asked in her old, craggy voice.

"Yes," he replied. "My brother stopped in for a visit."

Her head peeked in, and Uncle Garrick waved to her. "Oh, I didn't know you had a brother," she said, her eyes narrowing.

"Well, you never asked," he chuckled, then stepped outside for more privacy. It didn't matter. I could hear him even if he whispered. "Ms. Gingrich, I'd like to ask a favor."

"What is it?" she asked.

I was just about to rebut when he said, "I'll be taking Eris with me out of town for a bit, to visit the family. Would you mind watching over the place while we're gone?"

"Of course," she replied, patting his hand. "But you watch her well, Piers. Keep her safe."

"I will, ma'am. And thank you."

She nodded, then wobbled away.

Internally, I squealed.

My father had agreed to me going, but with strict rules. Mess up, and he'd drive me right back to New Mexico to stay with the Grinch, no questions asked. The utter seriousness on his face gave me no choice but to willingly agree.

Within a few hours, we were packed and ready to leave. Outside were two large, identical black trucks. To my surprise, Uncle Garrick had a Chevy Silverado 4x4, just like my dad's. I guess the Blaekthorn brothers were a lot alike.

Before we left, I saw Ms. Gingrich talking to Lyra. Lyra handed her a pamphlet, and then walked away. That was odd.

By the time we hit the highway, it was a little after midnight, and I fell asleep.

I dreamed of my brother. We were both younger, around the ages in the picture Uncle Garrick brought, and were playing in the snow. Behind us was a two-story log cabin with gray smoke billowing from the chimney. On the porch, my mom and dad sat with two steaming mugs in their hands, watching us. My father looked so much younger and stress-free. Smiles adorned their faces as they chatted and laughed with each other. I could see the love in their eyes, every time their eyes met. A look I'd never seen in my father's eyes.

Camden threw a snowball, hitting me directly in the face, and I stood there, stunned.

"Get him back, Eris!" my mother yelled. Her eyes were wide and kind, urging me to fight back.

I bent and gathered snow in my gloved hands, packing it into a tight ball. As soon as I threw it, Camden ducked, and I missed. Mom and Dad set down their mugs and ran out toward us. A family snowball fight began. Me and Mom against Camden and Dad.

My mother's laughter was beautiful. Like a ray of sunshine on the cloudiest day. We were laughing and screaming, chasing my dad and brother all around the front yard, throwing snowballs, tackling each other, making snow angels, and having a blast.

"Eris," my dad said, nudging me awake softly. "You okay?"

"M-hmm," I hummed. "Why?"

"You were making sounds in your sleep. Were you dreaming?"

"Yeah," I breathed, my heart still aching at the new memory. "I think my memories are starting to return." I was glad they hadn't come all at once. I wasn't sure if my heart could take it.

"That's good," he said.

I sat up and yawned, stretching my arms over my head. "Where are we?"

"In Colorado."

"How long have we been driving?"

"Almost seven hours," he said, his eyes tired. "I'm hoping we'll arrive soon."

We were still following Uncle Garrick's truck down a winding, narrow, bumpy road. A rocky cliff was on one side, and it looked like a sheer drop on the other. Snow lined the sides of the road, and I found myself white-knuckling the truck's grab handle.

"Haven't you learned to trust my driving yet?" he asked with a smile.

"On a normal road, yes. But in the middle of the boonies, on a road with snow, possible ice, and a death drop . . . my faith is being tested."

Dad laughed out loud, and it was a wonderful sound. I hadn't heard him laugh much since we moved to New Mexico.

He took hold of my hand. "Change is coming, Eris," he said, his eyes still on the road ahead. "But we'll get through it together, like we always have."

I turned to him and smiled. "I know we will, Dad . . . like we always have."

CHAPTER 3

A little after eight in the morning, we pulled in front of a building with a sign on its front that read "Havenwood Falls Medical Center." It looked like it was once a one-and-a-half-story home that had been renovated, and was painted white with blue trim.

Lyra waved goodbye and headed to a car in one of the stalls. Two men, who looked like they could be related, met my dad and uncle outside of the facility. Uncle Garrick extended his hand to the older one, who was wearing a flannel shirt and jeans.

"Sheriff Kasun," he addressed him, then nodded to the other, dressed in a police uniform. "Conall."

"Eris, why don't you go inside," my dad instructed. "We'll be right in."

It was cold outside, so I happily obliged.

As I stepped into the facility, I saw a girl around my age sitting behind a desk to the right, flipping through a magazine. She was pretty, with long black hair, hazel eyes, and a nose piercing. "Hi. How can I help you?" she asked with a smile.

I swallowed and walked up to her. "I'm here to see my brother, Camden Blaekthorn."

She gasped, her eyes widening as she took in my face. "Your Cam's sister, Eris." I was a little taken aback she knew who I was, but nodded. "Gosh, you've, like, totally changed since the last time I saw you."

I studied her face, but didn't recognize her.

"You, don't remember me, do you?"

I shook my head. "I'm sorry."

"Hey, it's fine. I suppose you'll, like, remember all the details later, huh?" She grinned, tapping the side of her temple with her finger. "My name's Taylor."

"Nice to meet you, Taylor," I said.

"I bet the family's glad you're back," she added.

I shrugged. "I haven't seen them yet."

"Oh." Her eyes flitted to a chart on her desk. "Well, I'm sorry about your brother. I hope they, like, find out what happened to him soon." She leaned over the desk and pointed to my left. "He's in room number two. Take a right around that corner, and it's down the hall on your left. The nurse practitioner checked on him like ten minutes ago, so you're free to go in."

"Thank you," I said.

"Good luck." She smiled. "And it's good to have you back."

I nodded and smiled back, then began my journey down the stark white hall. My heart hammered harder and faster with every step I took, a mixture of anxiety and excitement welling up inside of me.

The place smelled sterile, a mixture of bleach and lemon cleaners.

Then, I spotted a small black number attached to a door. *Two.* Taking in a few deep breaths, I placed my hand on the knob and paused. My feet were frozen, not allowing me to step any farther.

Just do it, Eris, I urged myself.

I took in one last breath, then turned the knob and pushed the door open.

A young man lay on a bed, eyes closed, chest steadily rising and falling. Wires were attached to him, monitoring his heartbeat. The steady spikes on the monitor appeared to be strong.

I studied his profile, his features so foreign, yet so familiar. Flashes of memories, once stolen from me, started to return. But they were from when we were much younger.

I still wanted to know why we'd been separated and all memories of him erased. They said it was to protect the town, but there had to be more. My dad left this place for a reason. What was so important that a father would leave his son? What happened here in Havenwood Falls that made us leave seven years ago?

I made a silent promise to myself, and to my brother, that I'd help to find out what happened. Even if I had to look myself.

Judging by the photo, Camden had completely changed. He wasn't a boy anymore. He was a young man. He looked muscular, his body a lot longer, his face thinned out, his nose strong, and jaw more prominent and stubbled with facial hair. I wondered if he would have known me if he saw me. Because if I'd seen him in New Mexico, even if he stood right in front of me, I would have never guessed he was my brother.

"*Who* are *you?*" A deep, sensual voice rumbled behind me, making me jump.

I turned back, but had to look up at the figure standing behind me.

Good God, he was gorgeous, around my age, with a strong jaw and straight nose. His hair was dark brown and unkempt, like he'd raked his fingers through it a few times. He was tall, at least six-one, with broad shoulders and defined muscles under his almost too-tight shirt.

But it was his eyes that captured me. Beneath the long, dark lashes were the most beautiful hazel eyes rimmed in gold.

Where did he come from? I hadn't heard anyone walk down the hall.

A devilish grin grew on his full lips, and heat rushed to my cheeks. Quickly, I turned away, arms crossed over my chest, hoping that if I ignored him he'd go away.

"Are you Cam's new girl?" he questioned.

I gasped, pivoting back to him. "Excuse me?" I shot him my best evil eye. But it did absolutely nothing, only made his full lips turn up even more—lips I wasn't sure whether I wanted to punch or to know what they felt like pressed against mine.

Wait. No! What the hell was I thinking?

He stepped closer, his right hand braced against the doorframe, blocking me in. "So, where has he been hiding you?" His voice was low and seductive, his eyes sweeping down my body and back up until he met mine.

"Who the hell are you?" I sneered, wanting to smack that adorable grin right off his face.

"I'm Cam's best friend, Rylan. Rylan Gilles." He held out a hand to me, but I didn't take it. I exhaled and turned my attention back to my brother.

"Well?" he pressed.

"Well, what?"

"Are you going to tell me your name?"

"No."

Laughter rumbled behind me.

I didn't know this guy and wasn't here to make a new friend. All I wanted, was to see my brother.

I heard him take a step closer and could feel his body heat radiating against my back. I twisted my head toward him. "Haven't you heard of personal space?"

His eyes narrowed as he tucked his hands into his jeans. "You're feisty."

"Well, you're rude."

"I like feisty."

"I'm sure you do," I exhaled. "So why don't you go somewhere else and find a feisty girl who gives a damn." He didn't respond, so I glanced back. "What?"

"Nothing." His eyes narrowed, studying mine, but he still had that damn snarky grin.

My dad's voice echoed from down the hall.

"Over here," I called, hoping to squash this awkward chatter.

"Hey, Rylan," Uncle Garrick said as they stopped near us. "How's Cam doing?"

"Nothing's changed," Rylan replied. "Vera said you'd gone out of town, but wouldn't tell me why."

Uncle Garrick smiled. "Well, this is why." He threw an arm around my dad's shoulder. "Rylan, I'd like you to meet my oldest brother, Piers. Cam's father."

"Wow," Rylan exhaled, extending his hand. "It's a pleasure to meet you, sir." My dad took Rylan's hand and shook it firmly.

"Piers, Rylan has been staying with me and Vera," Uncle Garrick explained.

I stayed tight-lipped but listened intently.

"He came wandering into Havenwood Falls about six months ago, after he lost his family. He and Cam became close friends, and when Cam told us about his situation . . . we couldn't help but take him in." He slapped an arm around Rylan's neck. "He's a good kid, and a big help around the property and the store."

"It's nice to meet you, Rylan," my dad said, using his cautious voice. I could see his eyes carefully studying Rylan's face.

"And," Uncle Garrick's hand landed on my shoulder, "Rylan, this is my beautiful niece, Eris . . . Cam's sister."

There was a sparkle in Rylan's eyes as he glanced at me. "It's a pleasure to meet you, *Eris*." His head angled, giving me a broad smile, revealing straight, white teeth.

God damn it. Why did he have to be so damn handsome *and* cocky?

We must have held each other's stares for some time, because my dad cleared his throat. Rylan turned away first, and I exhaled a breath I wasn't aware I was holding.

"I'm sure my brother has a set of rules for his household," my dad started, and my stomach began twisting. My dad glanced at me, and I knew exactly what he was going to say next. The same thing he told every boy he thought showed the slightest bit of interest in me. "But I have one very important rule for you. My daughter is off limits." It wasn't only a command; it was a warning.

"Yes, sir," Rylan answered with a nod of his head. He then glanced at me, and I shrugged, quickly turning away.

"Good, then," my dad said. "Now that we're all on the same page,

I need to see my son." He stepped around me and headed toward my brother. I tried to follow, but my feet were still frozen.

Uncle Garrick stepped forward, patting Rylan on the shoulder. "I'll see you at home." He then followed after my dad.

Twisting my head back one last time, I saw a smile broaden on Rylan's face, making the gold around his eyes shimmer brighter. He leaned close, his scent refreshing and attractive, a mixture of pine and fresh air, and what I thought the forest might smell like after a rainstorm.

"I'll catch you later, cupcake," he whispered softly into my ear, the heat of his breath brushing against my cheek.

"Don't call me cupcake," I growled. And before I could say anything else, he winked and walked away, chuckling, as if my dad's words meant nothing. As he exited, my body relaxed.

What the hell was wrong with me?

I turned my gaze back into the room. My father was leaning over my brother, whispering words into his ear, holding his hand. My heart ached as I finally stepped inside and closed the door.

CHAPTER 4

here was a knock on the door a few minutes later. A man walked in and shut the door behind him. He was of average build, with salt-and-pepper hair and navy-blue eyes. He tucked a pen into his white lab coat and walked up to my dad, extending his hand.

"You must be Piers Blaekthorn," he said. "It's nice to meet you. I'm Dr. Underwood."

My father took his hand and shook it. "Nice to meet you, Doctor. Do you know what's happening to my son?"

"We're not entirely sure. The mages believe it's a spell, and because my own healing abilities don't seem to work on him either, I'd have to agree. It's a dark spell that is keeping him in a deep sleep, and he hasn't been responding to any treatment. But Garrick told me about what happened to your wife. Do you know if—"

"Wait," my dad interjected, holding up his hand. He then turned his attention to me, and his eyes softened. "Eris, could you please wait outside for a moment?"

"Why?" I was confused. Was what happened to Camden connected to my mom?

"Please, honey." His eyes begged. "There are things we need to discuss privately."

"If it's about Mom and you know what happened, I think it's time you told me."

"I will, sweetheart," he said, his fingers brushing the side of my cheek. He stood in front of me, laying both hands on my shoulders. "I promise, when we're done here, and I know more, I will tell you everything."

"Everything?" I questioned.

"Everything."

"You promise?"

"Yes, I promise."

"Okay," I sighed, giving in.

He leaned forward and kissed my forehead. "Thank you."

I guess waiting a little while longer was better than nothing. I knew his memory was still returning too, so I didn't want to push him.

"I can take her home," Uncle Garrick offered, his eyes finding mine. "Your aunts Vera and Lydia are there and very excited to meet you. They've been going on about how great it will be to have another female around."

My dad's brow raised at me . . . a silent question to see if I agreed. And I did. I was glad to learn I had two aunts. Maybe they knew my mom. And maybe they would have some information about her to tell me.

"When you're done with the doctor, text me," Uncle Garrick said to my dad. "Lyra said she was going to register you with the Court of the Sun and the Moon, but I'll try to get a hold of her daughter, Addie, about putting on your tattoos. Maybe she'll be able to swing by the house later."

"That'll be great," my dad replied, his voice strained.

"Wait. Tattoos?" I said a little too excitedly, knowing my dad would never let me get one.

"They're temporary. For visitors," Uncle Garrick explained.

"Why?" I asked. "That's an odd thing to give visitors."

"This town is . . . well, not your normal town," Dr. Underwood added.

"Yeah, that's what I've been hearing." I exhaled.

Uncle Garrick's phone chimed. "Come on, princess," he said, glancing at his phone. "Aunt Vera wants me home. Something about a clogged pipe." He sighed and rolled his eyes. "I'll take you to your place, so you can unpack, or rearrange your room, or do whatever it is you want to do."

"We have our own place?"

"Of course you do." Uncle Garrick took my hand and led me out of the room. "We have cabins on the outskirt of town, where we run our business."

I glanced back at my dad before the door closed, his eyes sad, his body tense as he turned to the doctor.

What was really happening? I hoped he could find answers soon. I needed them as much as he did.

As we drove in silence, Uncle Garrick finally spoke. "Hey, Eris?"

I knew the tone. It sounded so much like my dad's voice when he was preparing to offer a "helpful" speech.

"Yeah?" I answered.

"I know this is a huge change for you. But we're all family, and you and your dad were meant to be here with us. I understand why your dad left and took you away from here. It was a hard time for all of us, but I really believe things will be better now that you're both here."

"You know what happened?"

"Yes." He sighed, deeply. "But that's not a story for me to tell. I'm sorry. I know your dad will explain everything soon, but I know it's overwhelming for him too. Everything he wanted to forget, all the negative memories, especially of the loss of your mother, has come back to him all at once. Just give him a little time to process it all." He placed his large hand over mine. "Okay?"

"Okay." I looked out the window and watched the tall pine trees pass by.

"It's good to have you back, princess."

"Thanks." I wondered if they all had their own nicknames for me.

In no time, we pulled down a road that headed toward the

mountains. On the left was a large building, with a sign on the front that read "Blaekthorn Lumber & Supply" around a logo of a howling wolf with pine trees. The entire building was decorated with icicle lights and other Christmas decorations.

"That's our family store," Uncle Garrick said, pointing toward it. "I'll give you a tour later."

"Wow, it's big," I murmured, more to myself. "I like the logo. Are there wolves in the forest?"

He laughed and glanced at me. "Yeah, there are definitely wolves that roam around this area."

"Oh," I replied. Dad would probably give me a weapon before I went sightseeing. "So, where do you get all the lumber?"

"Right here, on our property. One day we'll show you the operation. How we chop the trees, load them, and take them to our mill, where we strip and cut them into lumber."

I was impressed. "How big is the property?" It must have been huge to process a lot of lumber for a lumberyard. I also knew it took years and years to grow a tree.

A smile widened on his face. "Big enough. You'll soon learn about how things work here at Blaekthorn Lumber, but I think it's best if you and your dad, once he returns, sit and discuss more important matters first."

I nodded. His words brought nothing but more confusion, and made my head throb.

We traveled down a graveled drive, with manicured shrubs and greenery lining the path on either side, and beyond that, lots and lots of pine trees.

I imagined the drive filled with blooming flowers during the spring and summer. But it was winter now, New Year's Eve, and remnants of a recent snow lined the sides of the drive. The sky was brightening, but still gray and cloudy and cold.

Maybe I'd get to see snow fall before we left here. It didn't happen often in our small town in New Mexico.

Soon, three large log cabins came into view, each separated by at least a half-acre. They were beautiful, with snow-covered mountains as a backdrop. Pine trees in each of the front yards were covered with Christmas lights. I could barely see them now that the sky was brighter, but knew they'd be gorgeous at night.

The cabins were built the same—two stories, with front stairs that led to wrap-around porches. These were *not* what I had expected when Uncle Garrick said cabins, but then again, I recalled the picture and the dream I'd had, and they were exactly the same.

We pulled up to the house in the middle, where Uncle Garrick's truck idled. "Well, this is it. Welcome home, Eris." He handed me a key and patted my hand. "Cam has been staying here for the last few years, when he's not at our house for food, but we've made sure he kept the place clean. Your room is upstairs. I'm sure you'll know which one it is as soon as you see it. Your aunt Vera bought you some new bedding and girly room stuff, and said she can take you shopping later in town if you needed anything else."

"Thank you." I tried to smile, but wasn't sure if I was ready.

"Did you want me to walk you in?" he asked.

"No, I've got this," I said with feigned confidence.

"All right. When you're ready, come over. My house is that one." He pointed to the cabin on the left when his phone chimed. "Your Aunt Vera just texted. She'll have breakfast and coffee ready when you arrive."

"That sounds great. Thanks again." I grabbed my bag, and as soon as I slid out of his truck, a cold breeze bit every exposed area on my body. I shivered, ready to take Aunt Vera up on shopping for some warmer clothes, if I was going to be here for any length of time.

As he pulled away, I stepped up the stairs, stairs I probably ran up and down countless times in my past. My heart hammered, and I suddenly wished my dad was here. There were buried memories I had of this place, and I hoped they didn't come with some horrors.

Putting the key into the door, I twisted the knob and pushed it open. The inside was nice and open. To the right was a large kitchen with all the amenities, even a large potted poinsettia. Behind the kitchen was a dining area, and to the left was a family room with plush brown couches, a fireplace with a fire already crackling inside—most likely thanks to one of my aunts—and a large screen TV. In one corner was a large, real Christmas tree, beautifully decorated, but losing some of its needles, which were scattered on the ground under it.

Everything was rustic, logs and hardwood, with brighter rugs and curtains. The décor was warm and inviting, and gave me a real homey feeling.

Directly in front of me were stairs leading to the second floor. I headed up to find my room, starting with the room directly at the top of the stairs.

Turning the knob, I pushed open the door and clicked on the light. There was no doubt it was Camden's room. The décor was dark, with lots of blacks and deep reds. It was clean and somewhat organized, which I didn't expect. His walls were covered with rock posters and girls in bikinis, which, I guess, I did expect.

I was about to turn around and leave when I noticed something peeking from behind his pillows. I walked over to his bed and moved them. His headboard had four deep gashes, claw marks, marring the wood.

What the hell had happened?

I ran my fingers along them, and they were rough. Maybe he carved them out with a knife.

I didn't think he'd appreciate me being in here without his permission. But I also wondered if there was something here that could help me find out what happened.

On his dresser were a couple of pictures in frames. I picked up the first one, of Camden and Rylan sitting in front of a campfire roasting marshmallows. They were laughing, and it made me smile. I wondered what kind of a person my brother was—was he kind and fun to be around, or was he a jerk?

There was another picture of him on a ski slope with a snowboard in his hand. Next to him was a pretty blond girl. They were standing side by side, each with an arm around the other's waist. Another broad smile adorned his face.

In these pictures, he looked so happy, and the big question

lingered in my mind. Why didn't he want to come with us? Why did he want to stay?

Placing the pictures back, I turned to find my room. I headed down the hall to the door closest to Uncle Garrick's house. As soon as I opened it and stepped in, there was no question it was mine, but I felt like I was walking into a toddler's room. The walls were a pale pink, reminding me of cotton candy. They must not have been painted since we left.

Then, I noticed the bedding and the matching curtains.

Oh. My. God.

The comforter was pink and covered with images of *cupcakes*. The pillowcases were cupcakes, and so were the throw pillows. One had the word "sweet" written on it in silver sequins; the other had sprinkles and a cherry. Not to mention the matching cupcake curtains.

Internally, I groaned. Rylan lived next door and probably saw Vera come home with all this stuff. Hence, the "cupcake" nickname. Oh, God. I would never hear the end of it.

The carpets were a dark brown, like chocolate, and super soft. On one wall was a dresser, and on the other, a closet and another door.

Opening the door to the adjacent room, I found a bathroom— again, fully stocked with everything I needed. It was awesome, but I moaned at the décor. More cupcakes. The carpet next to the tub was a giant freaking cupcake. And the shower curtain—pale pink with cupcakes across the center. *What the . . . ?*

Aunt Vera had OCD—obsessive cupcake disorder.

The sound of a rumbling engine had me exiting the bathroom and peeking out my bedroom window. A motorcycle pulled into Uncle Garrick's driveway, and I watched Rylan's tall, muscular frame slide off the bike and pull off his helmet. Even from behind, he looked hot. Especially his butt, and the way it filled out his jeans.

After raking his fingers through his thick hair, Rylan's head twisted in my direction, his head lifting, his eyes finding my window. A broad smile rose on his lips, and then . . . he waved.

I snapped the curtain shut and pressed my back against the wall.

Crap! He caught me. How did he know I was watching? Did he know this was my bedroom?

The thought of him helping my aunt decorate my cupcake room was disconcerting.

Slowly peeking back out a small crack in the curtain, I watched him enter the house. My insides twisted, realizing he was going to be there when I went over for breakfast.

He was going to be trouble.

CHAPTER 5

*A*fter taking a shower and changing into my warmest clothes, I walked next door and nearly froze to death. How the heck could Rylan ride a motorcycle in this frigid air?

As I knocked on the door, my stomach somersaulted, over and over. For me, these were brand-new family members. Most of my memories still hadn't returned, and I was beginning to wonder if they would.

As soon as the door opened, I was squeezed tight by a woman I assumed to be Aunt Vera. She was beautiful, tall and lean, with long brunette hair and deep green eyes. "Eris Blaekthorn. Look at you," she said in a Southern accent. "You're all grown up, and so beautiful," she gushed, holding my face in her hands. "You look so much like your mother." Her smile was refreshing. "Come inside, you must be freezing."

"Thank you," I said.

She took my hand and led me into the kitchen where it was warm, and there was a huge spread of pancakes, bacon, sausages, hash browns, fruit, muffins, and coffee.

"Here ya go," she said, handing me a plate, pushing me toward the food. "You must be famished."

I wasn't gonna lie. "I am." It all looked yummy, so I decided to take a little of everything.

"Welcome home! I hope you like your bedding," she added. "There weren't many choices in town. It was either the cupcakes or a huge rainbow with clouds."

"I like the cupcakes," I said with a smile, sitting at the dining table.

"Well, good," she chimed. "I liked the cupcakes too. I thought the chocolate ones went perfectly with your carpet."

"They do," I agreed, trying to sound thankful. "Thanks again."

"Cupcakes?" a familiar voice sounded. "I love cupcakes."

I turned to see Rylan jogging down the stairs, freshly showered. He was in jeans and . . . shirtless. His upper body was still wet, glistening, and it looked as if God himself might have chiseled that chest. Tight skin. Muscles. Perfection.

A tribal tattoo covered his right shoulder and bicep.

"Rylan, put your shirt on," Aunt Vera puffed. "We have a guest."

"I see that," Rylan said before he stretched a shirt over his head. I watched in awe as his muscles flexed as he slowly pulled his shirt down.

Holy hell.

Before he spotted me gawking, I snapped my head to my plate, attempting to spear a stray strawberry.

"Rylan, this is Eris, Camden's sister," she introduced, plating a fresh batch of muffins from the oven.

Rylan's eyes met mine, with a sparkle in them. "Yeah, we met at the medical center."

Walking over to the counter, he grabbed a plate and piled on bacon, eggs, sausages, and pancakes. Then, he headed in my direction and sat directly across from me.

He winked, and I instantly felt self-conscious, wondering if I had food on my face or in my teeth.

"Rylan, how is Cam doing?" Aunt Vera asked. "Have they found out anything yet?"

"Nothing yet," Rylan replied. "But Sheriff Kasun and his pack have been investigating. Hopefully, the mages can find a cure soon."

"I hope so too. I've been worried sick. I'll drop by this afternoon," she said.

"What did you mean by pack?" I asked Rylan. "And aren't mages sorcerers?"

"Oh." Aunt Vera turned with a bewildered look on her face. "He meant officers, and I guess you could say the ones helping are like shamans. Healers."

The phone rang, and my aunt stepped out of the kitchen.

Rylan leaned across the table to grab the syrup, which was right in front of me. "Hey, cupcake."

"Don't." I scowled, which made him chuckle.

His head cocked to the side. "I thought you liked cupcakes."

"I do. I—" He was getting me tongue-tied, so I changed the subject. "You could have asked me to pass the syrup."

"And miss a chance to get closer to you?" he purred.

I narrowed my eyes, glaring at him, but my stomach had butterflies slam dancing inside. He picked up a piece of bacon, his eyes locked on mine, and he bit it. Damn him. And damn the way he made eating that piece of bacon so freaking sexy. He knew it too. *Jerk.*

Aunt Vera returned to the kitchen.

"Where's Uncle Garrick?" I asked.

"Oh, that was him. He'll be here shortly. He had to run over to the warehouse because they had a big order and needed his help."

"They should have told me. I could have helped," Rylan said.

"Oh, it's already done. Garrick just needed to operate the loader, and you know how much he loves driving that large machine," she said, turning with a grin.

"Hello?" A voice called from the door.

Aunt Vera shuffled toward it, wiping her hands on her apron. "Lydia, come in!"

"Is our princess here?" a high voice squealed.

In walked a pretty, blond woman of medium build, with bright red lips and large boobs. She peeled out of her long coat, revealing a sundress with brightly printed flowers all over it.

How could she not be cold?

Aunt Vera tipped her head toward me. "She's having breakfast with Rylan."

I heard Rylan chuckle under his breath, then I turned to watch Aunt Lydia enter.

"Eris, darlin'. Look. At. You," she gushed, clapping her hands in front of her. "You're a vision. Isn't she a vision?" Aunt Lydia also had a Southern accent, much stronger than Aunt Vera's.

I stood as she walked over, and she pulled me into a bear hug. My cheek pressed firmly against her chest, and I caught Rylan trying to swallow a laugh.

"I'm your aunt Lydia," she finally said, setting me free. "I used to change your diapers when you were just a baby." Another chuckle from Rylan. "You'll get to see your uncle Barney soon. He's been out chopping trees or God knows what else. I swear, if I didn't promise him food and some good lovin', that man would live in them woods."

"Lydia," Vera scolded, her eyes widening.

"Oh, Vera. Look at her. She's not a child anymore. Are you, Eris?"

"No, ma'am," I answered, feeling childish, and didn't dare glance up to see Rylan's expression.

"You'll also get to meet your cousins, Weston and Drake. They're over at a friend's house playing video games." She sighed. "I haven't seen much of them over winter break, but told them they had to come home this afternoon for our New Year's Eve barbecue."

She walked over to Rylan and gave him a hug. "I see you've met our resident hottie," she said. "He doesn't have a girlfriend yet. Well, at least none we know of." Her eyes narrowed on him.

Rylan shook his head. "No ma'am. No girl, *yet*." As he spoke the last word, his eyes met mine, making my face and insides heat. *Jerk*.

"Lydia," Vera scolded. "No matchmaking in this house. Piers will go full wolf on you."

I laughed. "Full wolf?"

They both looked at each other. "Oh, it's just a saying. Means he'll shred her to bits."

"Yes." Lydia laughed, slapping a hand on Rylan's shoulder. "Eris's daddy is wildly protective. We like you, Rylan, and your handsome face. So, don't go making googly eyes at her or make her blush in front of him," she warned, pinching his cheek.

This time *I* laughed as his nose crinkled.

"I'll keep that in mind," he said, his smile widening. "At least on my part."

"Eris, don't mind your aunt Lydia," Vera sighed, finally grabbing a plate. "She doesn't have a filter, and speaks whatever is on her mind."

"Don't worry." I chuckled. "I'm used to it. My dad doesn't have a filter either."

Breakfast was eventful. Both aunts asked me a ton of questions about growing up in New Mexico, and although there wasn't much interesting to tell, they hung on every word. Much to my surprise, so did Rylan.

"So, Rylan, what are your plans for the rest of winter break?" Aunt Lydia asked, popping a grape into her mouth.

"I'll probably ask the Kasuns if they need any help with the investigation."

"That's great. I'm sure they could use it. The sheriff and the Court have been extra busy this winter break, especially with that teenage girl who went missing . . . Heidi Bennett. Did you know her, Rylan?"

"No, but everyone in school was talking about her disappearance. It's almost been a month."

Aunt Lydia shook her head. "That's so sad. I hope they find that poor girl. Maybe she left and didn't tell anyone." Her eyes narrowed as she turned to Rylan, "Do y'all think Camden and Heidi's cases are related?"

"I don't know," Rylan replied. "They are totally different, but could be. Something strange is going on, that's for sure. I hope they find out what it is before anyone else goes missing or gets hurt."

"Yes, no going off into the woods alone," Aunt Lydia said, sipping her coffee.

"What happened to Camden?" I asked. "I mean . . . who found him and where?"

Rylan set his fork down. "A guy named Rusty found him in the woods and brought him into the medical center. He said he found him unconscious."

I nodded, wondering how it happened. "Where did he find him?"

"On the other side of Cooley Creek, which runs between the Blaekthorn property and Havenstone," Rylan replied, pointing east. "His body was found a few miles behind Havenstone. Right on the bank of the creek."

"Thank God for Rusty," Aunt Lydia sighed. "Who knows what would have happened to Camden if he hadn't been on patrol?"

There were stomps on the porch outside, and then we heard, "We're home!"

The door swung open, and Uncle Garrick, my dad, and another man with a full beard stomped in.

"Well, well, look what the wolves dragged in." Aunt Lydia laughed. Both women stood and headed over to the men. "Piers, aren't you a sight for sore eyes," Lydia said, hugging him tightly. My dad hugged her back.

"It's good to see you too, Lyd," he replied, his voice tired.

"Piers," Vera squealed. My dad picked her up and twirled her. "It's good to have you back. I can't believe how grown up Eris is. She looks so much like Aurora."

A sadness washed over my dad's face as he looked at me. "Yes, she does. And it's good to be back."

"Did they have any new news about Cam?" Lydia asked.

"No. Nothing yet," Garrick replied.

"Well, go get something to eat before you all waste away," Vera said, waving the men to the table.

"Princess!" The man with the beard exclaimed, smiling broadly at me. He looked like a muscular lumberjack. He had to be my uncle Barney, because he danced toward me with his arms wide open.

I stood to greet him, and when he reached me, he wrapped his large arms around me and squeezed me so tight I thought I was going to explode.

He was taller than both my dad and Uncle Garrick. His arms were as big as tree trunks, and his chest was solid as rock. He smelled like fresh-cut wood and earth, and when he hugged me, his beard tickled my forehead.

"Barney, let the girl breathe!" Aunt Lydia exclaimed, smacking him on his arm.

He let go with a hearty laugh. "Princess, you look as pretty as your mother. Thank God," he said, nudging my dad.

Dad glanced at me and smiled. "Hey, I contributed to half of her looks."

"Yeah, I can see that. She definitely has your ears and neck." Another boisterous laugh burst from Uncle Barney's gut. My dad first growled at him, then joined in with his laughter, which was infectious.

I was happy to see my dad with his family, smiling and laughing. For so long it'd just been the two of us, but it seemed like he was falling right back into this world. Although it was still a world without my mom.

I wasn't sure if any of the others noticed the slight sadness behind my dad's eyes, but I did. I knew him best, and also knew that being here was bringing back both good and bad memories.

While Aunt Lydia and Vera chatted with my dad, helping to fill his plate, Rylan stood and leaned toward me. "Catch you later, cupcake," he whispered, then took his dish and walked to the sink.

"Where are you off to, Rylan?" Aunt Vera asked.

"I need to run my bike to the Havenwood Falls Garage. It's making a weird noise, so Joshua said he'd take a look at it for me."

"That's mighty nice of him," she replied. "Well, be careful. There might be ice on the roads."

"Will do," he said. He glanced my way and winked before slipping out the door.

When he left, I felt a little sad and wondered if he'd escaped to avoid conversation with my dad. If I was him, I would have.

Aunt Lydia stood. "Eris, your aunt Vera and I need to run into town a little later. We need a few more supplies for the New Year's party tonight. Would you like to come with us? We can show you the town, and maybe get you some warmer clothes?"

"I'd love that." I immediately turned to my dad for affirmation.

"Yes, that's fine," he said. "As long as you stick with your aunts. No going off on your own." He gave me his very stern, serious look.

"I won't," I said.

"Eris, we have a lot to discuss," he added. "You ready to go home?"

The room instantly quieted. I stood and took my dad's and my dishes to the sink. "Thanks for breakfast, Aunt Vera. I'm glad I got to meet all of you . . . again," I said, and they all laughed.

I followed my dad outside.

"Hey, remember we're having a New Year's Eve party at our house tonight," Uncle Barney called after us. "We're gonna have a barbecue, fireworks, and I got a brand-new guitar."

"We'll be there," my dad said, then took my hand. "You ready?"

I took a deep breath and exhaled. "Yeah. I'm ready."

"Good, because it's time for you to learn the entire truth."

Even though a few memories had returned to me, I knew there were still things hidden without the spell. Like how my mom died, why I was taken away from this place, and why Camden was left behind.

I was anxious, but glad I was finally going to get some answers.

CHAPTER 6

The walk back to our cabin was short and brisk, but the cool air was enlivening. Walking up the steps to the porch, my dad paused and turned around to glance at me. I gave him a nod of affirmation and realized it was the first time he'd been back here since we'd left seven years ago.

He unlocked the door and pushed it in, then stood in the entry a few moments before he strode into the kitchen, toward the fridge, and opened the door. It was fully stocked.

Grabbing a bottled water, he twisted the top off and slid onto one of the barstools at the counter, then patted the stool next to him.

My heart thrummed inside my chest. Answers. I was finally going to get answers.

"Have all your memories come back yet?" I asked.

He took a swig and nodded. "Most of them."

"Mine haven't."

His eyes met mine. "They will. You were young when we left, so there might be things your mind won't remember."

I nodded. "What happened to Mom?"

He placed his bottle of water on the table and folded his hands together, staring blankly at the poinsettia in front of him.

Then he began. "Your mother was special. She was not only

beautiful, but she was brave and smart. And she loved her family fiercely."

My heart swelled at the thought. "How did you two meet?"

A memory must have flashed before him, because he blinked it away and took another sip of water.

"Before I explain anything else, there are things I need to warn you about. Things you might not fully understand or even believe in."

"Dad, just tell me," I sighed. "I promise . . . I can handle it."

A grin rose on his lips as he swiveled his chair to face me. "Your mother was a woman of magic, and she came from a long line of magic."

"Magic as in—"

"Witches," he said. "Your mother was a very powerful witch, as were her mother, grandmother, and great-grandmother. Her father—your grandfather—was a hunter." I was still trying to process the witch part when he added, "A werewolf hunter."

My eyes narrowed on him. "Werewolf hunter?"

I thought he was joking and started to laugh, but his face hardened.

Oh my God. He was serious.

I swallowed a lump in my throat. "Did he catch any?"

He turned away from me, his elbows resting on the counter. "Yes, he did. He was responsible for killing a mother and her thirteen-year-old son while they were out hunting for food one night. He shot the mother with an arrow, and when the son refused to leave her side, he shot him too."

"My God," I gasped. My heart ached as my mind conjured the horrific scene. "They were werewolves?"

He nodded. "Shifters that had taken their wolf form during the blue moon."

I swallowed hard. "So, what does this have to do with you meeting Mom?"

"Everything," he replied. "The pack—of the woman and boy—found out what happened to them and planned revenge on your grandfather. One night, when your grandparents and mother were sleeping, they attacked. They kidnapped your grandfather and mother, but your grandmother managed to escape. To this day, no one knows what happened to her. She just . . . disappeared."

"Do you think she's dead?"

"It's likely," he breathed. "If she was alive, I'm sure she would have tried to make contact. But we've heard nothing."

"And you met Mom . . . "

"They took your grandfather and mother deep into the woods where no one could hear their screams. Then, the man whose wife and son your grandfather murdered beat to near death and then bit Aurora —your mother and his only daughter—sealing her fate to become a werewolf. The one thing he hunted and hated most. Then, they beat him and ripped him to shreds.

"Thinking she'd die, they dumped your mother's body in the river. But they didn't know how strong she was. She drew on every bit of strength she had left inside, and clawed herself to the bank." He pressed his thumb and forefinger to the bridge of his nose. "That's where I found her."

A tear trickled down my cheek. "You were her hero."

He sighed, his brow furrowed, his eyes deeply saddened. "She was barely alive. We didn't think she'd survive through the night. My father called a shaman in a nearby town, and he did what he could. And before the shaman left, he pulled me to the side and told me my fate was tied to hers.

"I stayed with her the entire night, made sure she was breathing, and tended to her wounds. My mother didn't want to have anything to do with her at first, because she didn't want trouble with the rival pack. But she came around, after seeing how dedicated I was to keeping her alive."

"Rival pack? Wouldn't that make you . . . "

"Yes, Eris. My family—our family—are shifters."

I swallowed the huge lump in my throat, my heart jackhammering. "Werewolves?"

"Yes."

"The entire family?"

He nodded. "They are all werewolves. Your uncles, aunts, and cousins."

I sat there for long minutes, processing it all. The changes I went through when I turned sixteen, the dream of the woman with the wolf. It started to make sense.

I'd read enough werewolf books to know the heightened senses were part of it, but I'd always thought they were pure fiction. It was no wonder my dad was always asking me if I felt anything unusual. He knew I might experience these things. All that time I'd just thought he was being overprotective.

But in some of the stories I'd read, the wolves shifted at will, while in others, their shifts were controlled by the moon.

"Dad, can the family shift whenever it wants?"

"Our shifts were controlled by the moon and its phases," he started, and I cut in.

"Why haven't I ever seen you change or even be affected by the moon?"

He pulled his necklace from inside his shirt and held it between his fingers. I knew he'd had it for as long as I could remember, and he never took it off.

"This is an amulet. A Tiger's Eye stone. It is supposed to keep you grounded and stabilized, and enhances integrity and willpower. It is also a stone of protection. But *this* one is special." He rubbed it between his fingers. "Before we came to Havenwood Falls, your mother searched and searched, and found a spell that would allow us to change at will, and not be bound by the moon or its phases. Without the amulet, we would have no control."

"But, why haven't I shifted?"

"Most likely because you aren't a pureblood. Your mother was human—with magic in her blood—but she was not born a shifter. She was bitten. Most purebloods make their first shift by the age of thirteen. Those who aren't usually take longer . . . anywhere from the age of sixteen to eighteen. And I've even heard that some half-breeds never shift."

"Has Camden shifted?"

42

"He has. Garrick said his first shift was a few months after his sixteenth birthday. He was also given an amulet, but here, in Havenwood Falls, they have their own precautions. The tattoos given to the supernatural visitors and residents are magical. Another safeguard to keep the people here protected. For our family, it helps us keep our shifts under control. But with these amulets your mother spelled, we have an even greater advantage to live out normal lives, anywhere. Like we've been doing in New Mexico."

I pulled the pendant from around my neck and held it in my fingers. My dad had given it to me a year ago, when I'd turned sixteen. It was also a tiger's eye stone, in the shape of a heart, on a golden chain. He told me it was a gift from my mother and to never take it off. So I didn't.

"Your necklace was also charmed by your mother. To keep you safe and protected."

I looked up at him, his face solemn.

"What happened to her, Dad?"

"Once your mother regained her health and the new moon hung in the sky, we both transformed, shifting into our wolf forms. It was then I knew without a doubt she was my mate. The pull was strong, undeniable." He paused. "But, enough about that."

"Yeah, thanks. I don't want or need any details." I laughed.

"Your mother became my wife and mate, and we were very happy. But there was a threat we never knew of. A threat we never expected.

"A young woman, a close friend of your mother, saw how happy your mother was, and how happy we were together, and she became furiously jealous. I don't think she was in her right mind, because her obsession made her mad.

"The woman's mother was high priestess of her own coven, but she preferred to frequent your grandmother's coven and ceremonies. There were times she would follow us, hiding in the shadows, but we knew she was there. With the heightened shifter senses, we knew her scent and could hear her footsteps, even if we couldn't see her. At times, she would show up when your mother and I thought we were alone. It became very strange and uncomfortable, until one day, she caught me alone and off guard.

"I know you probably don't want to hear this, but that crazy woman tried to seduce me. I rejected her, of course, pushing away her advances, which infuriated her even more. She left in tears, ranting and raving about how I should have chosen her, and vowed that one day I would pay for my indifference and coldness toward her. I thought she was just a mad woman spouting meaningless threats and paid no heed. And we didn't see or hear from her after that day.

"Years later, we found this place called Havenwood Falls. We saw the kind of protection it offered its citizens, and how we could start a new life and business together as a pack. We settled in this area and made it our home. Being out in the woods, we decided to start the lumberyard business.

"After getting approval from the Court, your mother cast a growth spell over the forest. It makes the trees we cut down regrow to full size in weeks, instead of years. That's how our business can stay stable without leaving Havenwood Falls."

"Mom did a lot of good before she died, didn't she?"

"She did," he replied. "And she stayed true, all the way to the end." I stayed quiet, waiting for him to continue. It was just as hard for him to remember as it was for me to hear it for the first time.

"When your mother became pregnant with your brother, we were overjoyed. But when you were born, our family was complete."

"Dad, why did the picture on our mantel say that mom died giving birth to me?" I questioned.

"I wrote that because I knew I'd forget when we left, and didn't want to remember the truth of how she died."

"What is the truth?"

"I know it seems like I'm bouncing around the answer, but you need to know the entire story to understand."

"I know. I'm not pushing," I said, making a mental note not to keep asking him.

He smiled and continued. "I was walking out in the woods one afternoon when I heard footsteps behind me. I turned to see a woman standing in a long black robe, her face concealed within a large cowl. When she removed the cowl, fear overcame me for the first time since moving here.

"It was the woman. The crazed, jealous woman. And she'd somehow found us here in a place we thought we were safe. Her eyes were dark and evil, holding no emotion, and when I turned to walk away, my body froze in place. I couldn't move, and knew she'd cast a spell on me. I was alpha of my pack and protector of my family, yet this woman had rendered me helpless.

"Then, she offered me a choice. One *last* chance to leave your mother and start a life with her, or suffer the consequence. My temper got the best of me. I told her she was mad, and I would never love her. Then, I watched something inside of her snap. Her eyes went completely black, and I felt an evil power exude from her.

"Her mind was so dark and twisted, and there was nothing but hatred and jealousy in her heart, harbored all those long years. She stormed off, releasing me from the spell. When I chased after her, she was nowhere to be found. Not even a scent.

"I told your mother what happened, but we weren't even sure what she was capable of. What we didn't know was that she'd searched to find a specific spell, so dark and so evil. An unbreakable spell that would change our lives forever. Because I didn't choose her, I would now have to make another choice. To save the life of my wife or my daughter.

"It was on your tenth birthday when you and your mother fell ill. The mages here tried everything they could to stop the curse, to find a loophole, but they couldn't find one in this spell. They told me I had to prepare myself, because one of you would die." A deep sob ripped from my father's chest. His head fell onto his crossed arms on the table. My heart was shattering, splintering for the decision he had to make. Just the thought of having to choose the life of a loved one over another was devastating. It was no wonder he decided to leave this place. He didn't want to be haunted by the memories of that horrifying choice.

I reached over and took his hand, and he squeezed mine.

"I'm so sorry, Dad," I sobbed. "I'm sorry you had to choose between us."

Tears welled again from his bloodshot eyes. "Your mother made me promise to choose you. Made me swear to do everything in my power to protect you, to take you away and keep you safe." He paused and shook his head. "Your brother overheard me making the promise to your mother. He loved you, Eris, but he was just a boy who loved his mother dearly. He wanted me to choose her. Your mother loved you both fiercely, with every part of her heart, and proved she would give her life for either one of you."

"I don't blame him for wanting to choose Mom," I said. "If I'd known . . . If I'd understood what was going on, I would have told you to choose her, too."

"I know you would have." Dad gave my hand another squeeze. "The night before the spell took your mother's life—and half of my heart—Uncle Garrick found Camden in your room. You were sound asleep, and he was standing above you with a knife in his hand."

My chest constricted and ached. "He was going to kill me, wasn't he? Because he wanted Mom to live." Tears streamed down my face. "He must have hated me after she died. Hated that I was alive instead of her." I looked up at my dad. "And hated you for choosing me."

My dad slowly nodded. "I pray that no one else ever has to endure that kind of hell."

I finally realized why my brother had stayed. Why the family knew it was best, and why my father left him behind. And that day, my dad not only lost his wife and mate, he'd lost his son, too.

"I'm so sorry, Dad." I knew those words would never be enough to heal his shattered heart, but they were the only words I could find. "I have something to tell you," I said. Now that he'd told me everything, it was time I told him about me . . . about the changes and the dreams.

So, we sat at that table, and I told him everything, and when I was done, he hugged me.

"What ever happened to the woman who cast the spell?" I asked.

"No one knows. That day I saw her in the woods, she disappeared like a shadow, not leaving any trace of being in Havenwood Falls."

"Do you think she's responsible for what's happening to Camden?"

He shook his head. "I don't know. But I have to consider it a possibility."

"We'll get through this, Dad. Like we always have."

He smiled through his tears. "Yes, we will, sweetheart. Like we always have."

"So, now that all the secrets are out, what's next?" I asked.

"Lyra's daughter, Addie, will be coming to do our tattoos," he said glancing at his watch. "She should be here soon."

"Then what?"

"Then, I have to go meet Sheriff Kasun, and you're going to stay here," he said in his protective, fatherly tone. "We're going to team up, to try and find out what's going on." He swiveled back toward me. "I know your aunts are taking you shopping, but remember stay with them."

"Can't I go with you? I want to help."

"No," he said firmly, then sighed. "I know you want to help, but I don't want you anywhere near the woods. Not until we find out what's going on." His eyes softened. "Go have fun with your aunts. They're excited you're here. Okay?"

"Okay." I threw my arms around his neck, and he hugged me back.

"I love you, Eris."

"I know. I love you too, Daddy."

"I'm going to take a quick shower and change before Addie gets here."

I nodded and watched him leave.

I was trying to be strong. To show him I could handle all of this.

Outwardly, I'd become good at masking what was inside. But inside . . . inside I still had to deal with the overwhelming information about my family, who I was, and how I fit in. All while convincing myself that everything would be all right. My mother died to save me, and my brother tried to kill me. That fact alone made me wonder. Did Camden still harbor those feelings? Did he still hate me?

I'd have to prove to him that I was alive for a reason. I had to find a way to help.

CHAPTER 7

I was drowning in heaviness. Everything my father had shared with me—the secrets of who I really was, the curse, the promise, the reason my brother stayed—it was pressing me on all sides. The Blaekthorns were werewolves, my mother's side was witches, and her father a werewolf hunter. Talk about dysfunctional. So, what did that make me? And Camden?

My brother had already shifted, so he fit right into the Blaekthorn pack, but I was still in limbo. Maybe I would be one of those who didn't shift. Maybe I would embrace the other side of my heritage. I needed to find out more about my mother's lineage, the Witheridges, and where they came from.

A knock on the door made me jump. I thought it was the girl coming to give us the tattoos, but when I opened the door, Rylan stood there.

At the sight of him, my heart flip-flopped inside my chest, and I forgot to speak.

He laughed and raked his fingers through his hair. "I wanted to ask if, maybe later, you'd like to get a burger. Or whatever it is you like. There's a pizza joint in town, too."

I didn't know what to say. He was asking me to lunch, and we'd just met this morning. "My dad—" I paused, pointing upstairs.

"Yeah, I know. I just thought it'd be cool to get to know my best friend's sister."

God, he was making this hard. "I'm going into town with my aunts. But you're welcome to come by after, if my dad isn't here. The fridge is filled with food. I can whip something up?"

"You're going to cook for me on our first date?"

"Date?" I squeaked. "Definitely not a date. And I won't be cooking. I'll probably be throwing together sandwiches."

"That's fine with me." He shrugged, a crooked grin adorning his handsome face. "I guess I'll see you later."

"Yeah," I said, shutting the door behind him.

I let out a sigh of relief, thankful my dad wasn't here when he came to the door. Rylan was the first boy who'd heard his warning and still dared to come to my house and ask me to lunch. If my dad knew, he would never let me leave. Especially on a motorcycle with a boy I'd just met, who lived next door.

Later, my dad came down, freshly showered and changed. He was wearing blue jeans and a black-and-blue flannel shirt. "You look like you belong in a cabin in the woods," I teased.

"Well, I hope that's a good thing." He chuckled. A smile brightened his face. "I'm meeting the sheriff in town in half an hour, and I'm not sure how long I'll be gone. I told him I'd help, since he's gotten a few tips. I'll be checking out some areas while he talks to those who might have information. Uncle Barney will be coming with me, since he's the second in command. But Uncle Garrick will be next door, in case you need anything."

Not long after, a girl arrived at the house. She was very pretty, around five-six, in her mid-twenties, with light brown hair and brown eyes. She was dressed in black, with a diamond piercing in her nose and a bag slung over her shoulder. She introduced herself as Addie Beaumont, Lyra's daughter. She had come to give me and my dad our protection tattoos. It was strange, considering myself as something other than human. And it also made me wonder . . .

Was Rylan different? Did he have a protection tattoo, too?

Addie was a lot of fun and quick with her work. She did my dad's tattoo first, since he had to leave, and mine was next. Before she left, she told me that if I ever had any questions, I should come see her. It was great being accepted by the people in town, and I felt that maybe in the future, just maybe, Dad and I would return to Havenwood Falls and make it our home.

My dad grabbed his keys and headed for the door. "There is no ward on the property yet, so stay inside and keep the door locked. And when you go out with your aunts—"

"I know," I sighed. "I'll stay with them and be safe. And you be safe out there, too."

"Don't worry, sweetheart. I can take care of myself."

As I watched him walk toward his truck, Uncle Barney jogged from his house to meet him. "Hey princess, if you're bored, head next door. Your Aunt Lydia is starting her yoga session. It'll definitely keep you entertained." He laughed out loud before hopping into the passenger seat and shutting the door.

I giggled, watching them pull away. If Uncle Barney shaved his beard, he would be a mixture of my dad and Uncle Garrick.

And to think they were all werewolves. *Werewolves.* My entire family were shifters. What did they look like shifted? The thought was too overwhelming.

I closed the door and locked it behind me, then went to the fridge to see what kinds of things there were to throw together when Rylan came over. I was relieved to find cold cuts and veggies to make sandwiches. To the right of the fridge was a pantry, and inside I found some bread.

How long did they think we were going to stay here? The shelves were stocked with everything—cereal, crackers, canned goods. Then I remembered Camden was living here, too.

What was it like for him to have gone through his teenage years without a dad?

He truly missed out, because our dad had a lot of love to give. Yes, he was overprotective at times, but it was because he loved me to a fault. And I knew he would have loved Camden the same way. He still did. We were all he had left of our mother.

CAMEO RENAE

An hour later, my aunts collected me to go shopping. The drive into town was quick, but it was beautiful. The town was filled with lights and Christmas decorations. The shops were quaint, and it had that small-town feel and charm, and everyone we passed seemed so friendly.

We stopped at a few places, one where Aunt Lydia loaded up on fireworks, and then to a butcher shop where they bought steaks and burgers. For a break, we stopped at a quaint little shop called Coffee Haven. Inside, it smelled like heaven.

"Eris, would you like a coffee?" Aunt Vera asked.

"I'd love a mocha."

"You got it," she said. "After this, we'll walk to the Backwoods Sport and Ski shop, right around the corner. They have some warm jackets and thermals."

"Sounds good." I'd definitely need them.

There was a line, so while my aunts waited, I decided to sit by the window. Outside, I spotted a fountain in the middle of the square, and a gazebo. This area must have looked magical at night with all the twinkle and colored lights.

Out of the corner of my eye, I saw a glimmer of light pass by. I thought I was seeing things at first, until it zipped right past my window again, then returned, making circles directly in front of me.

I gasped, staring at the anomaly. It was my magic glimmer. It had followed me here, to Havenwood Falls.

I looked around the shop to see if anyone else noticed it, but no one did. Even the people it zipped around outside didn't notice.

It suddenly slammed into the window, making me jump, and then zipped away. It wanted me to follow, and the urge to get up and leave was strong. Then, my dad's voice was like a gong in my head. *Stay with your aunts.* Both of them were occupied, talking to other people in line.

Stay or go—that was the question.

To hell with it. This glimmer had been with me as long as I could remember, and always came when I needed it most. It was here for a

52

reason. So, against my dad's wishes, and in spite of the consequences, I stood and walked out the door.

The glimmer zipped around me, like it was happy I'd come, and then it started to move.

We went left down Main Street, passing Shelf Indulgence and The Haven Saloon. We kept going straight, right past the Havenwood Village Apartments. Then it took a right on Sixth and another left on Stuart Street. I had to remember these places in case the glimmer disappeared, so I could find my way back.

The frigid winter air was seeping right through my clothes, making me shiver. Down Stuart Street I began to pick up my pace to a jog. My aunts were going to freak when they found out I was missing, and I prayed they wouldn't call my dad.

This darn glimmer had better be leading me toward something important. As we came to the end of the road, I passed a park with a plaque declaring it Cook's Corner Park and right off it, I slowed and watched the glimmer enter a small graveled path . . . which led directly to the Havenwood Falls Cemetery.

A cemetery. Yep, I was dead. Especially when my dad found out.

Under a thick blanket of white, the cemetery was gorgeous. I could only imagine what it looked like in the summer with flowers and green grass, in its full glory. There were stone pathways, but no headstones, which was odd. But there were plaques with the names of the deceased on the stone walls surrounding me.

The glimmer led me down a maze of pathways, into different sections of the cemetery, farther and farther from the entrance. I started to second-guess myself when we finally reached a more secluded area and the glimmer stopped at the opening of a tunnel.

"Oh, hell no! If you think I'm going into that dark, creepy tunnel, you're crazy!" I huffed at the glimmer. Thank God no one was around, or they would have thought I was mad. It zipped back and forth in front of me. "No way. I'm not going in there." I stepped back. "I'm already in a crapload of trouble, especially when my dad finds out. I might as well pick a burial spot and start digging."

The glimmer zipped around me and then disappeared.

I was pushed forward, gasping as the glimmer touched me. Where it made contact was warm and tingly. It'd never touched me before. It usually just hovered around me.

It was suddenly back in front of me, glowing brighter, lighting the dark tunnel before me.

"You think that's going to help?"

It bobbed up and down as if it were nodding. This glimmer was sassy.

It zipped in front of my face, a foot away, just enough so I could focus on it. Its warmth surrounded me, making my fear and anxiety diminish.

"Fine," I exhaled.

What was the worst that could happen anyway?

The answer: There were too many horrifying things to even attempt to count.

The trip through the tunnel wasn't as daunting as I'd expected, and we reached the other side in no time. It exited into a wooded area, another cemetery.

I followed the glimmer until it stopped in front of a gravestone, and I noticed a large bouquet of fresh-cut red roses lying at its base. My body trembled as I made my way, finally standing in front of it.

A deep sob ripped from my chest, and my legs gave, dropping me to my knees.

"Mom," I cried, my heart shattering into a million pieces. I'd found her. My glimmer had led me directly to her.

My fingers traced the name on the headstone.

Aurora Witheridge-Blaekthorn
Devoted wife, mother, friend

And below that was another inscription.

Those we love don't go away.
They walk beside us every day.

Lying under the earth, right beneath me, was the woman who birthed me. Who loved and raised me, and even died for me. I wished I'd been given the chance to know her. And hoped that every single memory I'd shared with her here, good and bad, returned soon. I wanted them all. I wanted to remember and never, ever forget her again.

I knew the glimmer was near because I could feel its warmth radiating through me, like a warm blanket. But it did nothing to comfort me.

It wasn't fair. "I wish you were here," I wept, resting my forehead against her headstone. I missed her so much, and the ache in my heart was growing, making it hard to breathe.

Footsteps from behind made me jump to my feet and crouch in a defensive stance . . . something my dad had taught me.

I waited, my pulse racing, when Rylan stepped out of the woods.

I quickly wiped my tears and straightened. "What are you doing here?"

His hazel eyes met mine with a hint of concern. "Looking for you. Why? Aren't you glad to see me?"

I huffed, but wasn't going to lie. I was relieved it was him, and not someone—or something—else. "How'd you find me?"

"I have my ways," he said, stepping closer.

I crossed my arms over my chest and narrowed my puffy eyes. "Are you stalking me?"

A playful grin rose on his lips. "I don't need to stalk you, cupcake."

"What the hell does that mean?"

His head cocked slightly to the side as he tapped his left temple. "Intuition." He then took another tentative step closer. "But I think the bigger question here is . . . how did *you* get here? How did you find this place?"

There was no way I was going to tell him I followed a magical glimmer of light. So, I tilted my head slightly, tapped the side of my temple, and replied, "Intuition."

He threw his head back and laughed. "So damn feisty."

As he neared me, he slipped out of his black leather bomber jacket.

"You must be freezing," he said, laying it over my shoulders. The warmth inside his jacket seeped into my skin, instantly warming me. I pushed my arms through the sleeves and hugged it closer. His scent— his unique fragrance of pheromones mixed with hints of pine and wind—made my head tingle.

"Thanks," I breathed, my heart hammering at his closeness.

Glancing around, I noticed the glimmer was gone.

"I'm sorry about your mom," he said, standing next to me, facing her grave. "Your uncle told me what happened. She was brave and selfless."

I nodded, trying not to answer, because I knew if I did, I'd start crying again. As my eyes focused on the headstone, I noticed a subtle etching behind the words. It was of a wolf howling at a full moon, and within the moon was a pentagram. It was who my mom was, and maybe what I was to become. A wolf and witch.

"Why is she buried out here?" I asked. "What is this place?"

"This cemetery is for the supernaturals who live in this town. The other is for the humans." He paused for a moment, then glanced at me. "Just so you know, your aunts are freaking the hell out. Lydia called me, frantic, thinking you were kidnapped. They sent me to look for you, and if I don't get you back soon, she'll blow a major blood vessel."

Crap. "Have they called my dad?"

"Not yet. But the longer you're away, the more likely it is for those two to start gathering a search party." He chuckled.

"Do you have a phone? Can you call them?"

"Yeah," he said, pulling a cell from his back pocket and showing me. "But there's no service here."

Double crap.

"But they said they'll be waiting at Coffee Haven until they hear from me." He extended his hand. "Shall we?"

As soon as I took his hand, a current of vibration traveled from his to mine. I gasped, and his hand flinched, but neither of us let go. His hand was so warm, I didn't want to.

He quickly led me back to the entrance of the Havenwood Falls *human* cemetery, and sitting off to the side was his motorcycle.

Seriously, how did he know I was here?

Rylan hopped on his motorcycle. "Put this on," he said, holding out the helmet to me. I didn't argue. I walked up to him, took the helmet, and pushed it onto my head. It smelled like him.

"I've never been on a bike," I admitted.

"Just hop on the back and hold on."

"To what?"

His head angled to the side, and his smile became serpentine. "To me."

He turned on the ignition and revved his bike. I carefully slipped onto the back and wrapped my arms around his waist. I was so close, my front pressed up against his back. And I liked it. I leaned against him, letting his warmth seep through me.

"When we go around turns, just lean with me," he instructed.

"Okay," I exhaled. "What about your helmet?"

"I only have one. Besides, I have a thick skull." Before I could respond, he pulled out from the cemetery, making my grip tighten around him. He glanced sideways, a broad smile raised on his lips.

A car slowed as we traveled down Stuart Street, and Rylan slowed, too. As both vehicles came to a stop side by side, a guy around our age, with dark hair and eyes, rolled down the back window.

Rylan addressed him. "Hey, Kase."

The boy gave him a nod. "I was going to call you."

"What for?"

"We overheard a couple of human visitors say they saw Camden talking with two guys on black ATVs the night he was found. So keep an eye out."

"Thanks, man. I'll tell the family."

"No problem." Then Kase glanced at me. "Who's that?"

Rylan turned his head sideways. "Cam's sister, Eris."

"Eris?" His eyes widened as I gave him a nod, keeping my helmet on. I didn't want them to see my face, which was probably red, puffy, and splotchy from crying. "Welcome back," he said.

"Thanks." My reply through the helmet was muffled.

"I'm Will Kasun, or just Kase."

Kasun. The sheriff. This must have been his son, because I could see the resemblance.

"Hey, you guys coming to the Festival of Lights on January eighth? It's our first day back to classes," he groaned. "A group of us is meeting after school and heading up to Mt. Mae on the ski slopes. The views up there are killer. Much better than in town."

"We'll think about it," Rylan answered. "Thanks for the info. I'll catch you guys later."

"No problem," Kase answered, then waved as Rylan pulled away.

It wasn't long before we were back in town, pulling up in front of Coffee Haven. I slid off the bike and reluctantly took off the helmet, handing it back to Rylan. "Thanks," I said.

"My pleasure." His head nodded toward the store, where my aunts came rushing out, clearly shaken.

"Oh my God," Aunt Lydia exclaimed, throwing her arms around me, squishing my cheek against her boobs. She then pulled back and held the sides of my face in her hands. "What happened to you? Your face is all red and swollen. Are you okay?"

"I'm fine," I answered.

Aunt Vera hugged me next. "Eris, you were just about to send us to an early grave. What happened? Where did you go?"

There were eyes all around us, making me want to throw on Rylan's helmet and have him whisk me away. "I—I went to the cemetery to see my mom."

They both glanced at each other.

"Sweetie, you should have told us," Aunt Vera replied. "We could have taken you there after shopping."

"I know. And I'm sorry," I sighed. "I just felt like I needed to go there on my own."

"Well, you should have at least told one of us," she said, before her eyes softened. "But we do understand." I felt horrible that I left without telling them, and caused them so much stress. But I couldn't rewind the moment. "We have a few more places to stop before we head home. Did you still want to go to the ski shop?"

"Actually," I turned toward Rylan, "I was wondering if he could take me home. I'm really tired."

Rylan's brow rose. "Yeah, sure. I was headed home anyway."

"Honey, if your daddy found out you were riding on the back of a motorcycle with a boy, he'd not only kill us, he'd kill him."

"I promise, it'll be straight home. And I'll wear a helmet."

Aunt Vera stepped up to Rylan. "First, thank you so much for finding her," she said, laying a hand on his shoulder.

"No problem," he answered.

"Second, promise me that you'll drive super slow and safe, and take her straight home."

"I promise," he said, laying a hand over his heart.

"All right," she sighed. "He found you and brought you here safely. I trust him to take you home just as safely. I know you've had a rough few days. We'll finish up quickly and be home as soon as we're done." She dug a notepad and pen from her bag. After writing on it, she handed it to me. "Here's mine and Lydia's numbers. If you need anything, call us. But Garrick is home too."

"Thank you," I said, hugging them both.

I slid Rylan's helmet back onto my head and wrapped my arms around his waist as he started up the bike.

"Be safe! We'll be home soon," Aunt Lydia yelled as we pulled away.

CHAPTER 8

*A*fter a quick tour of the town, Rylan took me home. In no time, he pulled up to my front stairs.

"You want to come inside? It's lunch time, and I can make a pretty mean sandwich."

"Sure. Let me park this bike at home, just in case your dad comes early. And I'm going to tell Garrick what Kase told us."

"Who was that guy?"

"Kase is the sheriff's son. We met during football tryouts. At first, he was an ass, but when he found out what I was, he opened up. He was the one who introduced me to your brother. Even though Camden graduated the year before, they still hung out because they'd played football together. But Cam and I hit it off instantly . . . like two lost brothers finally connecting."

"That's cool," I said, handing him his helmet. I was realizing how much I missed out on Camden's life. He played football, but what were his likes and dislikes? Was he good at sports? I assumed he was, but had no idea. Rylan, a stranger before today, knew things about him I didn't, and it made me a little jealous. "I'll see you in a bit."

"Yeah, be right back." As he drove off, I ran up the stairs and opened the door, quickly ducking out of the cold.

A few minutes later, Rylan knocked.

"Come inside, it's so cold," I greeted him.

He stepped in, raking his fingers through his thick hair. "It's not too bad."

"Are you kidding me? I need to find the temperature control in here. It's freezing."

He stepped toward me, a lazy grin on his lips. "I'm hot blooded. I can keep you warm if you want."

I gulped. His closeness made my blood stir and ignited something inside. A heat. A warm, wonderful heat. I needed distance, so I stepped back.

"You don't have to worry about me, Eris. I'm not a big bad wolf." His eyes traveled to my lips, and I could barely breathe.

I hitched a thumb toward the kitchen. "If you're hungry, we have a bunch of sandwich stuff." I took another step away from his gravitational pull.

He noticed and chuckled. "Maybe in a bit."

"Okay," I exhaled. "Want to watch a movie?"

"Sure." He walked past me, deliberately brushing his arm against mine. *Jerk.*

I followed him into the living room, and he walked straight to a small cabinet under the TV. He knew the place better than I did, and I wondered how much time he spent here with Camden.

"What do you want to watch?" he asked, bending over. I couldn't help but notice his perfect butt. "Besides my ass," he laughed.

Oh hell. Embarrassment heated my face.

"Don't worry, cupcake. I don't mind."

"I wasn't . . . I—I'm going to get us something to drink." I swallowed hard, turning for the kitchen. "Water? Soda?"

"I'll take a Monster."

"A what?"

"Energy drink. They're on the door of the fridge. Second shelf."

"Oh," I exhaled. "Well, at least you know your way around this place."

He gave another wonderful laugh. "Yeah, this was my second

home. It was mine and Cam's place to get away from the adults and the twins."

"Are they bad? The twins?"

"Nah, they're cool. They're fifteen, but your aunt always asks us to keep an eye on them. I think they hate it as much as we do."

"So, you know about the Blaekthorns? About what they are?"

He popped his drink and took a swig. "Well, they don't howl at the moon like the shows suggest."

He did know. So, I pressed him.

"Did you get a tattoo when you came here, the ones for the supernaturals?"

He turned to me, his hazel eyes narrowed. "You can ask me anything, and I'll tell you the truth." He pulled his T-shirt over his head and turned his back toward me.

My breath caught in my throat at the sight. Yes, the almost invisible Havenwood Falls protection tattoo was there, but there was also another, covering his entire back.

Four large slashes were tattooed diagonally from his right shoulder down to the base of his spine. It looked like his skin was being torn apart from the inside out. At the end of the slashes were claws, dripping with blood. But there was something else, peeking from behind those slashes. A wolf, with golden eyes. And its eyes . . . they seemed so real, like they were peering deep into my soul.

My fingers automatically reached out to touch it, and as soon as my fingers grazed his skin, there was a current—a tingling heat, flowing from me to him. The muscles in his back tensed, making me gasp and pull away.

"I'm sorry," I apologized. "I didn't mean to touch it."

His head twisted to the side, the cocky grin back. "You can touch me anytime, and anywhere, you want."

Jerk, I thought. Only because I wanted to.

I was glad when he threw his shirt back on. "And in case you're wondering about the tattoo . . . it's a representation of the beast inside, waiting to be released."

"So, you're—"

"A shifter, just like your family," he answered, as if he were answering any other question. When I paused, his head twisted back to me. "I told you, I'll tell you anything."

"Why? You don't even know me."

He sat down on the couch next to me, the space between us instantly heating. "For one, you're Cam's sister, and your family has taken me in when no one else would."

I couldn't argue with his answer, and I wanted to know, "How did you find Havenwood Falls?"

He smiled, but the smile didn't reach his eyes. Instead, they held a sadness—a look all too familiar. One I'd seen many times in my dad's eyes.

"I came from a protective family and a strong pack. My father was alpha, but being the alpha's son didn't mean anything. Life wasn't any easier for me. From a young age, I had to prove myself . . . to work and fight for everything I got, and didn't get any special treatment.

"Over the past few years, our pack was targeted by rivals because of our strength. We could never settle in one place, so we became wanderers, moving from state to state for the safety of the pack. Even on the move, we still weren't safe. One by one, members were picked off, and our group was whittled down from twenty members to eleven." He turned to me, his face solemn. "About eight months ago, my father went hunting, and he never returned.

"The next morning, a few of the pack members found his body in the woods, shredded to pieces. No one knows who actually murdered him, but we suspected one person. A rogue shifter named Lars." The muscles in his jaw tensed, his eyes staring blankly at the wall. "Lars has been stalking our pack for years, waiting to find a weakness. Wanting to take over. He also had a thing for my mom. The bastard."

My heart ached for him. His story sounded eerily familiar, like my parents', only it was turned around.

"After my father's death," he continued, "his beta and best friend, Axel, took over the pack. Axel is a good guy and has been with my dad from the beginning. The entire pack trusts him."

"Shouldn't you have been the next alpha if you were his son?" I asked.

"I could have, but I didn't want the responsibility. After my dad passed, my mom wanted to leave the pack. She knew things would get worse, especially without my father's protection, knowing Lars was still out there. She felt that if she left, maybe he would finally leave them alone and the pack could survive.

"She asked me to leave with her. And I did. She was my mom, and I had become her protector." His eyes saddened. He leaned back, his head resting on the couch. I could tell that he was struggling with whatever he was going to say next. I could almost feel his pain.

"You don't have to tell me," I said. "Some things are personal, and I respect that."

He glanced at me, his hazel eyes narrowing. "No, I want to tell you. I want you to know my story." He paused, then looked away. "You know, so in case you think I'm a prick, you'll feel pity and cut me slack. Maybe even offer me some solace."

"Well," I said, placing my hand on his shoulder. "The only thing I'm offering you today is a sandwich."

He shrugged, a smile gracing his lips. "Then a sandwich will do."

Crossing one ankle over the other, he exhaled deeply, and I stayed quiet while he continued. "It was my mom who wanted to come to Colorado. She said she had this wonderful dream about a place where people like us could be safe." His eyes found mine again. "My mom had a gift. Her dreams were visions, and most times, when she had them, they came true.

"We were so close, not fifty miles away from this place, but we were starving. We found an old, abandoned barn to stay in for the night, and because she was so weak and tired, I insisted she stay and rest while I went and hunted for food." His eyes closed, and his jaw tensed again. "When I returned, I thought she was sleeping. I went to wake her, but found her throat had been slit." His brow furrowed, and tears welled in his eyes. He quickly turned away and wiped his face on his sleeve.

"Rylan, I'm so sorry." There were no other words. What do you say to someone who lost both of their parents in such a short period of time?

He shook his head, shaking the memory away. "Don't feel sorry for me, cupcake. I've learned hard and fast how to deal with life's twisted games. I'm a shifter. We adapt. We have to or else we die."

For some reason, I wanted to hug him. To wrap my arms around him and tell him I hoped his future was better. It could be, now that he was here. Now that *we* were here.

In the short time we'd spoken, I learned a lot about Rylan. That somehow, fate had brought him to Havenwood Falls. Fate had brought us all here, and we just had to figure out why we were chosen. Even if it was to live out our lives, knowing that there were others like us—different, but still searching for their place on this earth. A place where we all fit. And maybe, Havenwood Falls was that place.

I made us sandwiches, and we sat and watched a few episodes of Supernatural—something we both agreed upon—and after the episode was done, he stood and checked his watch. "I have to run to the warehouse and help them shut down early for the New Year's Eve barbecue tonight."

"The barbecue. Right." It would be the first time, as far as I could remember, that my dad and I would be celebrating the holiday with family. "Thanks for coming over," I said. "I really enjoyed the company."

A wide smile adorned his handsome face. "Thanks for listening. And, sorry about whatever happened in there earlier. I never spill my guts like that, or get emotional . . . with anyone. I guess you're easy to talk to."

"Well, I'm honored," I said and meant it. "Sometimes it's good to spill, you know, so you can fill yourself back up with good things . . . better things."

He nodded, considering my words. "A wise theory."

I shrugged, hoping he wouldn't regret spilling to me. "Will you be at the barbecue?"

"Good food and great company? I wouldn't miss it," he said, heading for the door.

I followed him, and without warning he turned and pressed his warm lips to my cheek. "Catch you later, cupcake," he whispered, his warm breath grazing my face, his lips lingering so close to mine. He'd rendered me frozen and speechless, then winked and walked away. *Jerk.*

I closed the door and pressed my back against it, my heart beating a mile a minute, while butterflies slam-danced in my stomach. The spot he kissed was still tingling and warm and . . . God, it was wonderful.

Rylan's good looks were one thing, but I was finding out there was a lot more to him than the prideful, snarky, testy jerk he first seemed to be. It would be hard to be normal around him, because whenever he was around, he made me feel things I'd never felt before. And there was no avoiding him. For God's sake, he was part of the family and lived next door.

Yawning, I realized how tired I was. The long trip last night and all the crazy events that happened today had taken their toll. I decided to take a nap before my dad got home. Besides, we'd be pulling an all-nighter to welcome in the new year.

Curling up on the couch, I clicked through the channels. The house was too quiet, so I needed the background noise. Especially being alone in an unfamiliar place.

The new version of Beauty and the Beast was on, so I left it and pulled a throw blanket over me. My eyes were heavy, and in no time, sleep had found me.

CHAPTER 9

"*E*ris. E—ris," *a female voice called, but the voice sounded hollow. My eyes opened, and I was on a couch. The TV was off, and the house was dark.*

"*Eris,*" *the voice called again.*

I sat up, getting my bearings, and realized I was at the house in Havenwood Falls. Feeling a bit frightened, I slowly peeked over the cushions. A bright light illuminated the top of the stairs, and I watched as it slowly hovered downward.

As the light reached the bottom of the steps, it grew bigger and brighter. So big and so bright, it was almost blinding. Then, it suddenly dimmed, and a woman stood in front of me, her body ethereal, illuminating the darkness around her. She was wearing a long white gown, and I realized I knew her.

"*Mom?*" *My voice trembled. Tears blurred my vision as I gazed into honey-colored eyes. Eyes that looked a lot like mine.*

"*Yes.*" *She smiled, her flawless porcelain face glowing. She was so beautiful, like I remembered, and was wearing a long white gown. "Don't be afraid, my darling," she replied. "Come."*

But I couldn't. I was frozen, my body trembling, my heart beating so hard and so fast I thought it might escape my chest.

It was the first time I'd seen my mom since we'd left. But I knew her face. I'd memorized it from the picture we'd had, and I recognized her smile. She had the brightest, most beautiful smile I'd ever seen.

"Come, Eris," she beckoned. "There is something I want to show you."

I gathered my nerves and stood from the couch. Yes, she was my mom, but my mom had also been dead for the past seven years, and now she was hovering inches off the ground.

I stepped toward her, and she waved for me to follow. Gently, slowly, she floated back up the stairs. When she reached the top, she turned right, and headed toward the only room I hadn't been in. My dad's room, and hers . . . once upon a time.

When she reached the closed door, she floated directly through it. As she passed through, it unlocked and creaked ajar. I slowly pushed the door open, noticing her glowing figure near the closet. The rest of the room was dark, in black and white.

"Come," she said, then pointed toward the closet door.

I walked toward the closet, and opened it. It was empty, aside from a few of my dad's dress shirts on hangers. She pointed to the left, and gave me a single nod. I leaned inside but saw a wall. A solid wall and nothing else. What did she want me to see?

"There's nothing here," I said, turning back.

Her hand was still pointing. "The floor, Eris. Look under the floor."

The floor was covered with carpet, but I dropped down anyway, on all fours, and tugged at the edge. To my surprise, it wasn't attached. It was merely a remnant laid on top. Tugging it harder, I folded the carpet back and crawled into the closet.

Then, like I'd seen in the movies, I rapped on the exposed hardwood floor with my knuckles. Sure enough, there was a spot that sounded hollow. Two of the boards had a slightly bigger gap between them, so with my fingertips, I pulled on the lip of a board closest me, and it came right up, leaving a dark hole in the floor.

Turning back to my mom, I watched her smile widen. "Take what is inside, Eris. It's yours now," she said, her voice angelic.

I sucked in a deep breath and reached inside. There was something hard and quite large, so I wrapped my fingers around it and pulled it out. Carrying it out of the closet, I took it to the bed and sat down where my mom was standing—hovering—and placed the rectangular shaped object on the bed. It was wrapped in a red cloth, so I began to unravel it.

It was a book. A leather-bound book with a pentacle—a circle with a pentagram inside—on its front. It was very old and smelled musty, and when I ran my fingers over the cover, the leather was soft, like velvet. I also felt something tingling inside my fingers when I touched it—a power pulsing within.

"What is this?" I breathed.

"A Book of Shadows," she replied. "It belonged to your great-grandmother, Margret Witheridge. It was her diary, so to speak, of all things she practiced. Her spells, herbs, potions, among other things. It was passed to her daughter—your grandmother, Gertrude—when she died. And then, it passed to me. It possesses spells—powerful spells, but mostly spells to protect and spells to heal."

I opened the cover, and on the bottom, written in old script, was:

Margret Witheridge – Salem Village, 1682

Goosebumps riddled my skin. "She was one of the Salem witches?"

"Yes." For the first time, her smile dimmed and her eyes saddened. "She was captured, tried, and found guilty. They hanged her while her husband and daughter watched."

A pain pierced my heart at the thought, and a stray tear trickled down my cheek and dripped onto the open page of the book. I watched the wet spot disappear, as if it were being sucked up. I touched the paper, and it was dry.

"The book has dried your tears," my mom murmured, and I felt oddly comforted.

"What happened after Margret died?" Since she was here, I wanted to learn as much as I could.

"After her death, your great-grandfather took Gertrude, and they left Salem, taking the book with them. Your grandmother treasured it, and entered her own spells she'd learned through the years. She later met and married your grandfather, and had me. When I came of age, the book was passed down."

"Dad told me what happened to you and Grandpa. I know he was a hunter and that you were kidnapped by werewolves and bitten in front of him. I also know they killed him and left you to die."

"That's true. But there was also a silver lining."

"Silver lining?" I huffed. "Your father was killed, you were beaten and left to die, and your mom ran away, never to be heard of again. Where's the silver lining?"

"If none of that had happened, I would have never met your father, and we would have never had you or Camden or the wonderful time we shared together. It was all a gift . . . the good that came out of the bad." She floated closer, and I could feel her warmth seeping through me. "I love you so much, Eris. I loved you the moment I knew you were in my womb, and even more the first time I held you in my arms and felt that magic pass between us. The very first time I looked into your eyes, I knew you were going to be special. Just like the rest of us Witheridge women. Yes, I loved you then, and I've loved you ever since."

"I've missed you, Mom," I said, my voice exiting in a sob.

"I know, my darling. But I've been with you, watching over you all these years."

Realization slammed me, like a brick to the face.

"You," I gasped, my eyes meeting hers. "You are my glimmer."

When she nodded, I lost it. My tears and sobs became uncontrollable, and my body wouldn't stop trembling.

"I've never left you, Eris. I've been with you all along."

Her words filled me, and wrapped around my shattered heart, attempting to mend it. How could I not know the glimmer was her? It was always there whenever I needed it most.

"Thank you," I finally said, after pulling myself together. "Do you know what happened to your mother? Did she die, too?"

"No," she answered. "When she heard I'd been bitten, and my father had been murdered, she panicked and ran. She was afraid, and I don't blame her."

"If she ran, how did you get the book?"

"When I was strong enough, I returned to the house and was surprised to find the Book of Shadows still hidden in a secret place only she and I knew of. It wasn't long after that when we made our way to Havenwood

Falls." She pointed to the book. "I've added my own spells onto the pages. But remember, these spells should only be used for good. Never for evil or for gain."

I nodded. I would never use a spell to harm anyone. "Dad told me about the dark magic that killed you. The spell that evil woman cast that made him choose between us."

"Yes, it was a very dark and very ancient spell. One that could not be stopped once it was sent," she said sadly. "But the woman had to give part of herself to the spell, and has paid for it."

"I'm so sorry," I sobbed. "I'm sorry he chose me."

"Don't be sorry, sweetheart. Don't ever be sorry. I would have always chosen you." Her hand reached for mine, but passed right through. "You are *my* life, Eris. You, your brother, and your father." As she came closer, I noticed her body was beginning to fade. "I don't have much time left, so you must listen carefully. The spell on your brother can be reversed. It was cast by a witch, who is attached to the woman who placed the spell against us long ago. It is being conjured out of revenge."

"Revenge? For what?"

"The woman who put the death curse on us is her sister. Because she had to give something to the dark spell, she offered her remaining power. But the spell took more than that. It took her beauty, leaving her face blistered and scarred.

"She twisted her story and told her sister—another powerful witch— that your father tried to seduce her, and that I had become so jealous I placed a curse on her. She lied and never told the truth. That she was the one insanely obsessed with your father, or that the dark spell she had cast was going to take a life.

"Her sister has come to avenge her. To make your father pay for something he didn't do. She spelled your brother, and her goal is to spell your father as well. A spell that will keep them in a deep sleep until they die."

Oh, God. I wasn't sure I could do this alone.

"There is no time, Eris. You must go, but remember, you won't be alone. She is right outside the boundary of Havenwood Falls, getting ready to cast her final spell against your father. She has two men helping her.

They came into Havenwood Falls and took something from your brother, which is how she cast the spell."

Oh, no. The two men. They must have been the ones the sheriff's son was talking about.

"I need to get in touch with Dad," I said, breathless.

"It's too late. She already has him."

My heart dropped. "What do you mean she has him? How?"

"The men. While he was out tracking down a lead in the woods, they knocked him out and have taken him outside of Havenwood Falls, just beyond the wards. She is heavily glamoured, but you can stop her, Eris."

"Me?" I gasped. "I can't stop her. I don't have powers, and I've never cast a single spell in my life. I wouldn't even know where to start."

"Eris," my mother whispered. "Everything you need is inside of you. Magic runs in your blood, and it will guide you. All you have to do is believe in it."

I was terrified. I'd just learned today, a few short hours ago, that I was part witch, and now I was supposed to stop a powerful, practiced witch on my own?

I looked into my mother's eyes and saw something that made me pause my thoughts. It was a look that only a mother could give. Unconditional love, trust, hope, and faith in her daughter. She believed in me, and I not only saw it . . . I felt it.

She leaned forward and rested her hand against the middle of my chest. A surge of power slammed into me, making me fall back.

Gasping, I sat back up. "What happened?"

"The power inside you has been awakened. Find the witch. Stop her. She has the spell that can reverse your brother's curse. As soon as it is broken, cast a spell of protection around the family. There is a powerful spell in the Book of Shadows. It was written by your grandmother. Find it, and speak the words, Eris. Speak them from your heart and feel them with your soul."

I nodded. I could do this. I would do it for my dad and for my brother. The evil witches had already taken my mother, but they weren't going to take anyone else in my family.

I could feel the power inside my blood start to churn. I could feel it growing, writhing, and coiling under my skin.

"How will I find her if she's glamoured?"

My mother placed her pointer fingers on my eyes and spoke, "See that which has been hidden. See the evil lurking in the shadows and bring it to light."

When I opened my eyes, I felt a buzz all around me.

"Find her, Eris. Find her before she spells your father. Once she curses him, she will disappear, and I fear you will never find her again."

I couldn't fail. My mother had given her life for me, and now I would prove that she saved me for a reason. It was my duty now to save my brother and my father.

"I'll find her, mom," I promised. "And I'll reverse the spell."

"I know you will, sweetheart," she said, reaching for me, but her hand passed right through. "I love you, Eris. I always have, and I always will. Remember, I will always be with you."

"I love you too, Mom." With tears streaming down my face, I watched her fade, until I was left in the darkness, alone.

CHAPTER 10

J shot up on the couch in the living room with a cooking show on the TV. I glanced at the time, and a few hours had passed. The sun outside was already starting to set.

"Dad?" I called, but the house was quiet. "Dad!" There was still no answer.

I peered over the back of the couch, to the stairs and wondered about the dream. It felt so real.

Real or not, I had to find out.

Jumping off the couch, I dashed up the stairs and headed straight for my father's room. Inside, the layout was exactly as it was in my dream. I walked up to the closet and pulled open the door, and another surge of déjà vu smacked me.

Dropping to my knees, I pulled the rug back—a remnant that wasn't tacked down. I found the two boards with the larger gap between them and pried the board closest to me open. Without thinking, I reached into the hole. My heart hammered as I felt the hard, rectangular object.

Pulling it from the hole, I sat back, holding the book wrapped in a red cloth. The exact red cloth I'd dreamed of. Overwhelmed with trepidation and excitement, I quickly replaced the board, threw back the carpet, closed the closet door, and ran to my room.

I plopped down on my cupcake bedspread and carefully unraveled the book from the cloth, and there, staring at me, was my great-grandmother's Book of Shadows . . . old and leather-bound, with a pentacle adorning the front.

I could feel the book, feel its power urging me to open its pages filled with magic. But I had one task. To find the spell—the protection spell—that would cover our family, written somewhere inside.

I flipped through the pages, the symbols and drawings calling to me to look and decipher them. To draw from the power of the words written within.

But not now. Right now, I had to stay focused.

As I kept turning, I noticed a section where the handwriting had changed. Where the ink looked a little fresher than the last entry. It must have been the start of my grandma Gertrude's entries.

I turned and turned the pages until I saw it. The protection spell. I could feel the page, feel the words as if they were jumping out at me. The spell was simple. The words powerful.

I quickly dug for my pen and notebook in my bag. I quickly copied the words of the spell, and tore the page out. Shutting the book, I could still feel its power. Feel every spell in the book, luring the power inside me, begging to be set free.

This book—this old, powerful book—was now my responsibility, and I would have to keep it safe and hidden.

A loud knock at the door downstairs sent my heart racing. Wrapping the book back in the red cloth, I tucked it away between my mattresses, until I could find a proper, safe place for it.

Racing down the stairs, I peeked from behind the living room curtain.

It was Rylan. He'd come back.

He was wearing blue jeans and a tight shirt. The sky was icy gray, and the wind was whipping. I ran to the door and unlocked it, letting him in. As it opened, a cold rush of air whooshed in. Rylan stepped inside and quickly shut the door behind him.

We were toe to toe, so close I could feel his warmth wrap around me. I took in a deep breath, because his scent was wonderful, that mixture of pine and fresh wind.

Snapping myself from the fog that had just entered the room, I took a step back, but my heel caught on the mat. I fell backward, but before I hit the ground, Rylan caught me.

I inhaled, folded over his arm, his body above me like he'd dipped me in a dance. There was a buzz in the air between and all around us. His eyes, the gold in them was so—

He broke his stare and then stood straight, pulling me upright.

"Thank you," I exhaled.

"You'd better watch your step, cupcake," he murmured, a cocky grin on his face.

My mind was still buzzing from being in his arms. "I have to go somewhere," I said, moving toward my jacket.

"Eris," he called after me. I started to jog upstairs and get my warmer jacket, but as my foot hit the second stair, he called my name with greater urgency. "Eris!"

"What?" I said, taking the third and fourth step.

"Your father is missing."

I froze, not reaching the fifth, but pivoted back to him. My worst fear was being confirmed. "What did you say?"

"I was next door when Barney came busting in. He told Garrick he hasn't been able to get in touch with your dad. Apparently, they were checking on a lead in the forest, but when Barney called for him, he wasn't there. He wasn't anywhere."

"What about his phone?"

"They tried, but he hasn't answered." His brow furrowed. "The service in this area is spotty. Sometimes it catches, but a lot of times, it doesn't," he added. "Both of your uncles just took off to look for him. They didn't want to tell you because they didn't want to frighten you. But I thought you should know."

"Oh, God." Tears slid down my face. My body trembled, my legs buckled, and I fell onto the stair. "It's true, then. She has him."

"Who?" Rylan asked, taking a few strides across the room to reach me.

"A witch. The one that spelled my brother. She has my dad and is going to spell him too. I need to find her. I need to stop her." I looked up at him. "And I need your help."

"What do you want me to do?" Rylan asked, his gaze softening. "I'm here for you." He held out his hand. "Just tell me how I can help."

I had to gather myself. This wasn't a time to break down. This was a time to prove my worth. To justify my existence.

I took Rylan's hand, and he pulled me to my feet. "I need you to take me to find her."

"You know where she is?"

"No," I sighed, hoping he didn't think I was mad. "But I think she's outside of the town's wards. Once we get on the road, I might be able to find the way." I really wasn't sure, but I hoped. With everything inside me, I hoped I could find them.

"All right," he said, nodding. "Go get your jacket, and meet me outside."

"Thank you," I said, then headed upstairs. I grabbed my warmest jacket, wishing I'd gone to the ski shop, and grabbed the paper I'd written the spell on, tucking it into my pocket.

Outside, Rylan was sitting on his motorcycle. As soon as I stepped out, he handed me the helmet, and I slipped it on and hopped on the back. I wrapped my arms around his waist as he started the bike.

The air was cold, and the sky was growing darker. I hugged him even tighter as the wind whipped around us.

"Relax," I heard him yell. But I couldn't. My body was tense, watching the trees whip by.

When we came to the main road, Country Road 13—aka Burdorf pass—he stopped.

"Which way?" he asked, the bike idling.

I closed my eyes. *Please show me. Lead me to Dad.* When I opened my eyes, I saw my glimmer shoot out from behind a tree. It zipped up to me and touched my cheek, giving me a warm kiss before it took off toward the left.

"Left," I said, and he pulled out.

Rylan maneuvered the bike with ease, and as we left the town of Havenwood Falls, I kept my eye on my glimmer.

It led us farther and farther away from the town, and just when I wondered if we were outside of the wards, the glimmer stopped.

"Stop," I hollered, and Rylan pressed his brake. I squeezed him tight as we skidded off to the side and he cut the engine. Sliding off the bike, I pulled the helmet from my head.

High up on the road were the headlights of someone coming into Havenwood Falls, so he pulled the bike off the side of the road, concealing it behind some trees.

"There is nothing here," he said, looking around. Nothing except the looming dark forest. But my glimmer was still here, zipping in and out of the tree line.

"She's here. The witch is glamoured, but I think I can find her."

"How? How are you getting this information?" he asked. "Not that I don't trust you."

I gazed into his eyes. "My mom," I answered. "She came to me in a dream, and told me what I needed to do."

He nodded and gestured to the forest. "Okay, then. Lead the way."

CHAPTER 11

I took a step into the trees, and the glimmer shot deeper.

"This way," I said, quickly following after it.

Rylan was on my heels, and I was glad he was here with me. I never would have made it this far without his help, and wouldn't have been as brave. Knowing he was a step away, I felt safe.

My feet stumbled a few times on matted roots, but I caught myself and kept going. Pressing on, I hoped I wasn't too late.

Find the witch. Stop her, make her reverse the spell, and then cast the protection spell around my family. That was my task, and I repeated it like a mantra, over and over.

Continuing to follow the glimmer, we went deeper and deeper into the woods, where the trees were tightly knit together. The branches scratched at my exposed skin as I pushed through.

Then, the glimmer stopped. I froze and held my hand up to Rylan; he paused and nodded his head.

I could feel it. A dark power nearby, its evil tendrils seeping out from its master.

The witch was close.

I closed my eyes and called to the power within me. To a power, new and raw, passed down through generations . . . through the Witheridge bloodline.

I felt that power. Felt it stirring in my bones and in my blood. Felt it flowing through my veins, and I welcomed it.

Show me the witch behind her glamour, and give me what I need to overcome her, I begged that power.

This time, when I opened my eyes, the world around me was different. It was glowing and alive. But ahead of me was a wall of darkness shaped like a dome. I saw the magic, the glamour, like a dark wave, and knew behind it was the witch. I could feel her.

Fear tried to strangle me, so I turned to Rylan. As if he could feel my fear, he stepped to my side and grasped my hand. That simple act gave me what I needed . . . told me I wasn't alone.

"Stay here," I whispered.

"Where are you going?" He held my hand firmly, keeping me in place.

"There is a ward, a dark dome of magic concealing the witch, right beyond these trees."

His eyes narrowed as if he were trying to see. "Where?"

"It's a glamour. You won't be able to see it."

"And you can?"

I nodded. "Just stay here. I'll be fine," I lied.

"No way. You're not going in there alone." A fire blazed in his eyes, which had now turned completely golden. The look was one I wouldn't argue with.

"Okay, but please be careful."

His head tilted to the side. "*You* be careful."

With his hand in mine, we stepped forward toward the dark wall.

Inside, I called to my power and felt it growing, tingling inside of me. I let go of Rylan's hand, taking a tentative step forward. Lifting my arms, a wave of light exploded from my palms, slamming into the glamour. The glamour shattered, sparks of magic fell around us like glittering rain, revealing four figures behind it. One was a woman standing in a black cloak, her face concealed behind a large cowl, a black wand in her hand.

As she removed the hood, her evil gaze was frozen on me, her eyes black as night. The sight of it made my skin crawl.

Standing behind her were two men, and between them, bound to a tree, was—

"Dad!" I screamed, running forward.

The witch snapped her wand at me, and its power soared toward me like lightning, slamming into my chest. It threw me backwards, my body crashing against a tree. As I fell to the ground, pain radiated through my chest. I gasped, trying to catch my breath, but it wasn't coming easily.

Behind me, a deep, terrifying growl cut through the night air. Then, a huge, brown wolf came bounding out of the woods, stopping at my side. He was beautiful. His golden eyes fixed on the witch with a predatory focus. Its lip curled back, revealing long, sharp teeth. But he was larger than any wolf I'd ever seen. On his four legs he was just as tall as I was.

"Rylan?" I breathed.

His head twisted back to me, and his golden eyes met mine. He whimpered, and I shook my head. "I'm fine," I exhaled, pulling myself to my feet.

He stepped closer, angling his body in front of me, protecting me. I ran my hand across his side. His fur was soft, and my palm tingled as I stroked him. "Thank you," I whispered. His head bowed before snapping back to the woman.

His body went rigid as the two men stepped forward with knives in their hands. Their heads were covered with black ski masks, only revealing their eyes.

The witch laughed. "What do we have here? A young witch and a wolf? Now that's something you don't see every day."

"Release my dad," I said as bravely as I could.

I tried to take a step closer to her, but the wolf wouldn't let me move. He pushed me back with the side of his head.

"Who are you to give me orders . . . girl?"

"I am not a girl," I roared.

The witch threw her head back in laughter. "Not a girl? Then what are you?"

I glared at her. "I am my mother's daughter. A Witheridge witch,"

I responded. I could feel the power writhing inside, growing, as if it agreed and responded to my words. "Release my dad," I demanded.

I placed my hand on the wolf and gently stroked his fur. He must have felt my power, because he stepped to the side and let me pass. His eyes still fixed on the threat, his growl deep and guttural.

A sly grin rose on the witch's lips. In a split second, she raised her wand again, but this time I was ready. I raised both hands, and as her power hurled toward me, it struck an invisible wall, instantly dissolving.

Her power didn't touch me, and I barely felt it.

The aghast look on her face mimicked what I was feeling. *I'd stopped her.*

Courage and hope surged inside of me, unfurling through my limbs, while confusion and rage swirled in her eyes.

Raising her wand again, she struck. Her power flew toward us like a ball of flame. I lifted my hands in front of me, and an invisible shield devoured that flame.

She tried again and again, hurling her power at us, trying to hurt us, but my power absorbed every blow.

"How?" she screamed in frustration. Then, her eyes narrowed on us. "Get them," she ordered, her long finger aimed at us.

The two men came charging forward, blades raised over their heads.

Rylan leapt in front of me, sinking his jaws into the first man's waist. With a snap of his head, the man went flying, slamming hard against a tree. When he fell, his body was still. I couldn't tell if he was unconscious . . . or dead.

The wolf then turned his attention to me, dipping his head, and without words, I knew what he meant. He was going after the second man, and he wanted me to go after my dad.

My dad was unconscious, blood dripping from a wound above his left eye. "Hold on, Dad. I'm coming."

The witch turned her attention to him and raised her hands, conjuring a solid wall of wind to surrounded both her and my dad. She was going to cast her spell.

I called on my power, whatever I had left, and pushed it toward her shield. But it had weakened, and I couldn't break through. *No!* There had to be a way to stop her.

A loud yelp made me turn to see the wolf on the ground, the hilt of a blade sticking out from his thigh. The man had escaped Rylan's hold, and his attention was now turned to me.

He sprinted toward me with a look of malicious intent in his eyes. I dropped to my knees and held up my arms in front of me, anticipating the blow. But it never came.

Instead, I heard a growl and a snapping of teeth, followed by an injured scream. Opening my eyes, I witnessed the man's left arm, trapped in the wolf's jaws. He fought back, slamming his fist into the wolf's eye. Then he jumped up, wrapping his legs around the wolf's neck, and squeezed.

"Rylan!" I screamed in horror.

But the wolf was strong. He thrashed his head side to side, slamming the man's head against a nearby tree. As soon as the man's grip loosened, Rylan tossed him into the air, and before he hit the ground, the wolf caught his leg in his jaws, and dragged him into the darkness.

I tried again, to summon the power within, but felt nothing.

"You think you can match my power, young witch?"

I was spent. The power I had called earlier had completely drained.

"She might not be able to, but *you* cannot match *my* power," a voice called from behind us.

From the darkness stepped a small figure, hunched over, with wiry white hair wound in a tight bun.

"Ms. Gingrich?" I blinked a few times, making sure my eyes weren't deceiving me. "How? Why are you here?"

Her eyes met mine. "Because, my darling, I have watched over you all these years, making sure you were safe, and I don't intend to stop now." She smiled, holding a white wand in her hand.

Was Ms. Gingrich a witch?

I watched the old woman step toward the evil witch with no fear.

The witch let out a deep cackling laugh and snapped her wand at the Grinch.

"No!" I screamed, but Ms. Gingrich didn't flinch. She raised her wand, easily deflecting the witch's strike as if it were a wisp of wind.

I watched in complete awe as the hunched old woman walked up to that wall of wind and held up her wand. In the blink of an eye, the wall disintegrated. With another flick of her wrist, the evil witch dropped to her knees, holding her neck as if she were being choked.

"You will release the spell from the boy and his father, or I will release the breath from your lungs . . . forever," Ms. Gingrich commanded.

The witch gurgled, trying to gasp for air. When she finally nodded, Ms. Gingrich released her. She fell to the ground, coughing.

"Do it now!" Ms. Gingrich warned, her wand hovering above the witch in warning.

Ms. Gingrich was even more powerful than I imagined. But a witch? How could I not know this?

I ran over to my dad and released his bonds. His limp body fell to the ground, still unconscious. I rolled him to his back and pressed my ear to his chest. His heartbeat was loud and strong. He was alive.

Rylan stumbled out of the woods, shirtless, wearing jeans that were a bit too baggy. I jumped up and ran over to him, blood seeping through the blue denim where he'd been stabbed. His left eye was red and swollen where the man had slammed him over and over.

"Are you okay?" I asked. It was nearly impossible to avoid admiring his perfectly sculpted chest and abs.

"Fine," he replied, jerking a thumb in the direction he'd come. "But you should see the other guy."

I wanted to laugh, but a thought shot through my head. "Is he dead?"

"No," he replied, with a crooked grin. "But he doesn't have any pants."

Shaking my head, I giggled. He took a step, but his injured leg gave. I caught him, wrapping my arm around his waist to hold him up.

His eyes narrowed. "You caught me," he said, throwing his arm around my shoulders. "I guess this means we're even."

"Yeah, I guess."

"Who's that?" he asked, his head tilting toward Ms. Gingrich.

"She's our neighbor from New Mexico." His eyes widened, and I shrugged. "Don't ask, because I have no idea."

I helped him over to Ms. Gingrich, who still had her wand hovering above the witch as she reversed her spell.

When the spell was finally undone, Ms. Gingrich looked at me and held out her hand.

"Come, Eris. The spell is broken. We have one more thing to do, together."

"How did you know?" I asked, still completely confused at her appearance.

Ms. Gingrich smiled broadly, then began to twirl her wand above her head. Magical dust fell over her, peeling away what appeared to be a glamour. Then, right before our eyes, Ms. Gingrich was no longer there, and in her place stood a tall, slender woman, with long golden hair, braided behind her back. She was wearing a white cloak, but had the same white wand in her hand.

"Who are you?" I asked, although she looked familiar.

Her brow raised. "Don't you know me?"

"You're the woman in my dreams," I murmured. I gazed into her honey-colored eyes and gasped as realization hit me. "Gertrude?"

She smiled widely. "I prefer Gertie. Gertrude makes me sound like an old woman."

My body went weak, and I grabbed on to Rylan's arm for balance. Was this really happening, or was I still stuck in a dream?

Gertie opened her arms wide to me, and as I met her, her arms enveloped me in a warm embrace. My body trembled, and tears flowed from my eyes.

All this time, my grandmother *had* been there, watching over me, glamoured as the Grinch.

"Why didn't you tell me?" I asked. "Why use a glamour?"

Her eyes filled with sadness. "I was afraid. I'd never met your father, and because I ran, after the wolves took your grandfather and mother, I was sure he hated me. I couldn't take the chance to be rejected." She shook her head. "I was a coward back then, but after I heard of Aurora's death, I vowed to watch over her daughter, the next Witheridge witch. I followed you and your father to New Mexico, glamoured myself as an old, nosey woman, and moved next door."

I was overwhelmed. Too much information was hitting me all at once.

"How did you find me here?"

"The brochure that nice lady handed me got me here, but a locator spell led me directly to you." I shook my head, still trying to process it all, when she held out her hand to me. "How about we finish this together, once and for all?"

"Do you really need my help?" I asked, after seeing how powerful she was.

She smiled. "Not really, but I figure it would be nice to do this together, since you made the promise to your mother."

"What?" How on earth could she know that? It was a dream.

She tapped the side of her head with her wand. "The Grinch knows much more than you think."

Oh crap. She knew her nickname.

In the middle of a dark forest, my grandmother and I—Witheridge witches—stood, side by side, hand in hand. The witch on the ground stayed there, unmoving. She'd felt the power of Gertie Witheridge, and she knew she was no match.

Together, we recited the spell of protection over our family, and together we ended the curse. My grandmother told the witch the truth about how her sister had killed my mother, and why. Then she offered a warning—that if she ever saw her again, hell would be unleashed on her and her entire family.

The witch walked up to my grandmother, her head dipped and eyes solemn. "I'm sorry about your daughter and furious my sister lied to me. After what she did and the lies she told, she deserves everything that has returned to her."

"We forgive you," Gertie said, taking hold of her hand. "Now go, and do good."

"I will," she said.

After gathering the two injured men, she left.

While my grandmother went to check on my dad, I went back to Rylan, my eyes darting to the wet crimson seeping through his jeans.

"We need to get you to a doctor."

"Nah," he replied. "It's already healing. By dinner, there will be nothing but a scar."

"Are you serious?"

He laughed, the muscles on his abdomen tightening. "Wanna see?"

His signature cocky grin was back, making my face flush with heat. I wanted to say yes, but shook my head instead.

There was rustling out in the woods. "Piers!" Voices called in the distance. "Piers?"

It was my uncles. "Over here," I yelled back.

In less than a minute, both of them pushed their way through the trees into our area, drenched in sweat.

"What the hell happened here?" Uncle Garrick asked, looking at all of us standing around.

"You missed all the action." Rylan chuckled, leaning back against a tree.

"What happened to you?" He pointed to the blood on Rylan's jeans.

"He got stabbed in the leg, defending me," I answered.

Rylan shrugged. "Battle wounds."

"By who?" Uncle Garrick's eyes turned golden, scanning the area.

"They're gone," I said. "And they won't be coming back."

"How?" he asked.

"It's a long story," I sighed.

Uncle Barney walked toward us. "You saved our niece, Rylan. You deserve an extra-large beef rib at the barbecue tonight."

Rylan pointed a finger at him. "Hey, I'll be looking forward to it."

"How did you find us?" I asked.

"We're family, and with Piers back as our alpha, we followed his scent," Uncle Garrick replied.

"Yeah," Barney cut in. "But if we'd have taken the truck, we would have gotten here faster."

"How would we have caught his scent while sitting in a truck?" Garrick grumbled.

Uncle Barney shrugged. "I could have hung my head out the window." Uncle Garrick groaned and shook his head.

"Eris?" my dad moaned. He was sitting up, a hand pressed to his forehead.

I let go of Rylan and ran to him, dropping to my knees. "Dad, are you okay?"

He nodded slightly. "Aside from the throbbing pain in my head." He leaned forward and grabbed me, pulling me into one of his tight dad hugs and kissed the top of my head. "I'm so glad you're safe."

"What happened?" I asked.

He paused, shaking his head. "Barney and I were following a lead in the woods, somewhere alongside Cooley Creek. I heard something behind me, and when I turned . . . I guess I was knocked out. I don't remember anything else after that." He glanced around. "Where are we?"

"In the woods," Barney answered. My dad moaned, clenching his eyes shut.

"We're outside of Havenwood Falls," I added. "A witch captured you and was going to put a spell on you, but we stopped her." I turned my gaze to Gertie. "*She* stopped her and made her reverse Camden's spell, too."

"Who is she?" My dad tried to stand, so I helped him to his feet.

"Someone I want you to meet," I said softly. Gertie had backed up and stood near Rylan. As we made our way toward her, their eyes met. "Dad, this is Gertrude Witheridge. But she prefers to be called Gertie."

"Gertie?" he exhaled, his eyes narrowing, a deep crease furrowed on his brow.

She stepped forward. "It's nice to finally meet you, son-in-law. In my real form."

Complete confusion riddled my dad's expression.

"Dad, she's Ms. Gingrich. She'd glamoured herself to look like an old woman because she wasn't sure if you'd accept her. Then, she moved next door to watch over us."

My dad's attention fell back to Gertie, his eyes studying her face as if he'd seen a ghost.

"It's true," she said. "I never had the chance to apologize to Aurora, to tell her how sorry I was for running away. But I was afraid. The wolves murdered my husband, and when I couldn't find her, I thought she was dead, too. So I ran. Ran as fast and as far away from that place as I could." Tears rimmed her eyes and spilled down her cheeks. "I'm sorry, Piers."

My dad shook his head. "Gertie, Aurora had already forgiven you. She never stopped loving you, and she understood why you ran." He took hold of her hand. "Thank you for watching over us and keeping Eris safe."

"It was my pleasure," she said with a smile. "I'm sorry for being so hard on you all those years as Ms. Gingrich. I was just being protective."

"I know," he said. "You don't need to apologize." My dad faced the rest of us. "How about we go home?"

"Sounds like a plan," Uncle Barney puffed. "If I don't get my big ol' rear in front of that grill soon, Lydia will kill me."

My uncles helped my dad back to Gertie's car along the roadside, while I walked with Rylan to his bike and helped pull it out from the trees.

"Can you ride this while you're injured?" I asked him.

A smile tugged at the corners of his lips. God, even in the state he was in—sweaty, dirty, his hair in disarray—he was still unbelievably handsome. How was that even possible? "Don't worry about me, cupcake. I'll be just fine."

I smiled, glad he was back to his cocky self.

My dad walked up to Rylan and offered him his jacket.

"Thanks," Rylan said, pushing his arms through it, covering his bare chest.

"Thank you, for protecting my daughter," my dad said, extending his hand. Rylan took it and they shook. "I will never forget it."

Rylan's eyes glanced my way. "It was my pleasure, sir. And I'd do it again in a heartbeat. But you should have seen her. She was pretty badass herself."

My dad's eyes narrowed at me, and I shrugged. "How about I tell you all about it on the way home," I offered.

He smiled, and nodded. "I'd like that."

All of us, except Rylan, piled into Gertie's small hatchback. On the way back to the cabins, I told them everything that had happened—about the glimmer, the cemetery, the dream of my mom, and finding the Book of Shadows. I also told them about Rylan coming over and offering me help, and when I was being attacked, how he shifted into his wolf and took out the two men. I told them about the power I had, and how Gertie came in the nick of time to save us all.

They were quiet, all the way back, listening carefully to every word I said.

"Your mother would have been so proud of you." My dad finally spoke, breaking the silence. Pride lined his voice. "And whether you shift or not, it doesn't matter to me."

"She will shift," Gertie cut in. "Her inner wolf is waiting to be released, but I've kept it calm and quiet over the past year. It's only a matter of time before she shifts."

My head whipped to her. "My dreams. They were true. You were lulling my inner wolf to sleep."

"Yes." She nodded. "I didn't think your first shift should have been in our quiet neighborhood, closely watched by its residents."

"No," I said. "Thank you for that."

We finally pulled into the driveway when my dad leaned forward. "Gertie, we would love it if you joined us for dinner, and help us usher in the new year."

"Yes," Uncle Barney chimed in. "We have more than enough food. And you're family, Gertie. You'll always be welcome."

"Thank you," she said kindly. "But there are a few things I need to take care of back in New Mexico. But you can be sure I'll be around. I won't miss out on my grandchildren's lives."

I leaned over and gave her a hug. "Are you sure you can't stay?"

"Yes. This time is for you and the Blaekthorns to bond. I've had a lot of years with you, as the Grinch." A smile widened on her lips; her hand patted my cheek. "Don't worry. I'll see you again soon."

My chest ached at the thought of her leaving. "Thank you. I couldn't have done it without your help."

"Yes, you could have. You're a Witheridge. We're strong and never give in. You would have found a way."

"I'll miss you."

"I promise I'll see you soon," she said, her eyes glimmering. She leaned forward and pressed a kiss to my forehead.

"Okay," I sighed. "I'll see you soon."

I gave her one last hug and watched her pull away. Then we headed to Uncle Barney's house for the barbecue.

"I need to call the medical center and the sheriff," my dad said. "But I don't have service here."

"Use our house phone," Uncle Barney replied.

I still couldn't believe everything that had happened in one day. It felt like I was still stuck in a dream. But this wasn't a dream. It was real. I had a family. A large family. And a brother and a grandmother.

Tonight, there would be so much more to celebrate than the new year.

CHAPTER 12

*A*s soon as we entered the house, the smell of meat, spices, and baked goods hit us, making my mouth water. Aunt Lydia and Aunt Vera had been busy in the kitchen all afternoon, oblivious to what had happened over the past few hours.

"Damn, Lyd," Uncle Barney said, wrapping his wife in his arms. "This house smells like heaven."

"It'd better. It had to lure you home, didn't it?" He threw his head back and laughed, then gave her a loud kiss. When he pulled back, he smacked her behind, and she yelped.

"Gross, dad," a boy walked in, rolling his eyes.

"Yeah, gross," another repeated, following behind him.

"Boys, come here," Uncle Barney said, wrapping his arms around each of their shoulders. "Weston and Drake, I'd like you to meet your cousin Eris and your uncle Piers."

They each smiled and shuffled toward us, hugging us awkwardly.

They were identical twins and handsome like the rest of the Blaekthorn men—dark-haired with dark features, their eyes flecked in gold. The only difference was one of them had slightly lighter eyes. They were still young, without muscles, but they were already taller than me.

"Don't worry, I still can't tell my sons apart," Uncle Barney laughed.

"Goodness gracious, what happened to you?" Aunt Vera gasped, looking at my dad's bloodied head.

"He got knocked out," Uncle Garrick explained. He headed to the fridge and grabbed a few beers, handing one to my dad.

"Yeah, what he said," my dad muttered, placing the cold bottle to his temple. "I'll be fine. I just need a painkiller, or four."

I heard Rylan's bike outside and went to the window. He'd pulled into Uncle Garrick's driveway.

"Hey, Barney, where's your phone?" my dad asked.

Headlights from a vehicle were headed down the drive. At first, I thought it was Gertie, but I was wrong. A large black truck pulled up right in front of the house.

Rylan noticed and headed our way. He was able to walk on his own now, with a slight limp.

"Dad," I called. "I think the sheriff just pulled up."

Everyone exited the house and stood on the porch as Sheriff Kasun slid out of his vehicle. Then they all went quiet as another figure exited from the passenger side.

My pulse started to race, and even with the chill in the air, I started to sweat.

"Oh my, it's Camden!" Aunt Vera exclaimed.

Seeing my brother, conscious, for the first time in seven years sent a wave of emotions coursing through me. I was happy to see him, but I was also nervous as hell. He'd hated me and wanted to kill me. He wanted my dad to choose my mom, instead of me. And I didn't blame him.

I stayed on the porch as everyone else ran down to greet him. He'd been here all these years, and had become like a son to them all.

I heard my dad ask Sheriff Kasun if he could come by and explain everything in the morning.

"Have fun with your family tonight," the sheriff said before jumping back in his vehicle. "I'll see you tomorrow."

As the family greeted Camden, Rylan came and stood by my side. He knew what happened between me and my brother, and I had a feeling he was standing beside me because he wanted to make sure I was safe, and that Camden wouldn't try anything stupid.

The family made their way back to the stairs, and as they reached the top, Camden stopped in front of me. He was tall, about the same height as Rylan, and handsome—a mixture of my dad and mom. His face held no expression, and it made my heart ache.

Rylan moved slightly, and Camden's eyes snapped to him, narrowing. "I see you've met my sister."

Rylan gave his signature grin and glanced at me. "I have, and she's pretty special."

I heard a growl rumble from my brother's chest before his eyes turned back to me with a harsh glare.

"Camden," I breathed, my voice shaky.

He shook his head, his brow furrowed, and my heart shattered. *He still hates me.*

Then, his gaze suddenly softened, and his fingers touched the side of my face.

"Eris. You've grown up," he said. Then, without another word, he grabbed my arms and pulled me into a hug. I hugged him tight and felt his chest heave.

Both of us stood there, in the cold, surrounded by family, and wept. Our hearts healing, mending, after all these years. When he finally let go, his bloodshot eyes stared into mine. "I'm sorry, sister. I was young and confused, and Mom was my world."

"I know," I breathed. "She was mine too."

"Can you forgive me?" he asked.

I nodded, tears refilling my eyes. "I already have."

He wrapped me in a tight embrace one more time. "Thank you." He pressed his forehead against mine. "I'll see you inside."

The family headed into the house, leaving me and Rylan alone.

"Hey," he said, his hand brushing against mine. "I'm gonna head over to shower and change."

I grabbed hold of his hand, halting him. "Thank you," I said.

"For what?"

"For being here."

He shrugged. "I was just making sure things were copacetic."

"Yeah, I know you were. But not only for that . . . for everything you did today. You were there for me, and I appreciate it." I rose up on my tiptoes and kissed his cheek.

A crooked grin lifted on his handsome face. "You don't think getting stabbed in the leg was worth a real kiss?"

"How about you take a rain check, for a time when my entire protective family isn't standing right on the opposite side of the door."

"I'll take it," he said, then winked and walked away.

THE BARBECUE WAS AMAZING, and everyone was stuffed and happy to be together again, as it should have been all along. We ushered in the new year, knowing change was imminent. But I was ready for it and welcomed it. We all did.

Over the next week, our family began to mend. My memories were still returning, but now it was time to create new ones. It was great having an older brother, who I found was just as protective as my dad.

On top of that, my dad decided to move us back to Havenwood Falls, where he would take his place as alpha of the Blaekthorn Shadow Pack and help with the family business. I also decided that I'd be enrolling the next year at Havenwood Falls High as a senior.

I really hoped my grandma Gertie would follow us here. But that was still uncertain. I was just glad to have her back in my life, knowing I could connect with her anytime I wanted.

Rylan and I spent a lot more time together, especially since winter break was still on. He was a senior at Havenwood Falls High and would be graduating soon, but he already had a steady job at Blaekthorn Lumber and Supply.

My dad let him get closer than any other guy had, and even let him take me out a few times, only not on his motorcycle. And Camden sort of tagged along.

For the first time in my life, I felt a sense of stability. That hole I'd had in my heart for all those years was steadily being filled. And I noticed it in my dad, too. Things were finally taking a turn in the right direction, and we were finally becoming whole.

IT WAS the eighth of January, the first day of school after the winter break, and the night before we had decided to head back to New Mexico to pack our things for the big move. It was also the night of the Festival of Lights—a time when the residents of Havenwood Falls gathered in the town and on the mountainsides, offering tribute to all those who had fallen and lost their lives while protecting the people of the town and its secrets during the massacre of 1876.

Rylan asked my dad if I could go, and because Camden and the twins were going, too, he agreed. After school, Camden and I met Rylan and the twins at the school, and drove up Mt. Mae. We were all given paper lanterns and lighters before we rode the ski lifts up the slopes. There, we met other students from Havenwood Falls High.

I recognized the sheriff's son Kase in a group of guys, and was introduced to Rowan, River, Zaltana, Julianna, Viv, Breckin, and Zara, who also rode the lifts up. It felt great to be a part of something, with kids my age, especially after being homeschooled for the past three years.

We made a bonfire between a few trees and waited for nightfall.

One of the kids explained to our group about the event. That it was meant to honor those who had given their lives for the town and its residents throughout the centuries. Also, every year on this same night, all residents of Havenwood Falls turned off their Christmas lights for the last time until the next season.

Not long after, we watched as the entire town below went dark, and then stood in a moment of silence.

I couldn't help but think of my mother. She'd sacrificed her life for me. Gave everything so I could live, and I was standing here because of her.

A bright red flare shot high into the sky from city hall, a sign for everyone to begin lighting their lanterns. Rylan held ours between his hands while I lit it.

I placed my hands over his as a cold wind whipped around us. Our eyes met; the panes of his handsome face illuminated from the lantern's warm glow.

"You ready?" he asked.

"Ready."

We let go and watched our lantern slowly ascend. Then, my glimmer appeared out of nowhere and circled around it. Seeing it, knowing it was my mother, knowing she was here to witness it, made me emotional.

Tears pooled in my eyes, blurring my vision as I watched the lantern lift higher and higher, along with the thousands of other golden-lit lanterns filling the onyx sky. It was unbelievably beautiful and so peaceful, and with the darkened town below, it was a wonder to be seen.

Then, as if the moment weren't already magical, wisps of snow curled and danced around us, and gasps and laughter filled the air.

I turned, looking into Rylan's eyes, and his gaze softened, making my heart burst. I placed my hand against his cheek, his fingers gently grazed against mine.

God, I loved the way he looked at me, when his eyes looked like molten gold.

I gnawed on my lower lip, which caused a low laughter to rumble from his chest.

He held the sides of my face, then slowly leaned in. The warmth of his breath against my cold cheek sent tingles down my spine and through my belly.

"I'm cashing in my rain check right now," he whispered, and I nodded.

Heat rushed to my core as his warm lips found mine, sweeping gently across them. I opened to him, and his kiss deepened, becoming intimate. At that moment, I was lost, a paper lantern floating high in the sky above.

"Hey, Rylan." Camden's voice yanked me from bliss and pulled me back down to earth. "Rylan!"

Rylan's lips lingered a bit longer before he pulled away. When we turned, there was a girl standing next to Camden.

"She's been looking for you," he said, hitching his thumb toward her.

The girl was around our age, very thin and tall, with long brown hair and dark brown eyes. She looked sickly and tired, with pronounced, dark bags under her eyes.

Still in Rylan's arms, I felt his muscles stiffen as the two of them stared at each other.

"Keira, what are you doing here?" he asked in a not-so-friendly tone.

"Rylan," she breathed, taking a tentative step forward, her head dropping. "The pack needs you."

"What are you talking about?" Rylan bit, "Axel is in charge. He's more than capable to run the pack."

"No, he's not," she said, her voice trembling. "Lars killed him, or at least we think it was him, leaving us leaderless. We've been on the run, trying to survive." Her hands twisted around themselves. "You're the rightful alpha of our pack, Rylan. If we don't get protection, we're all going to die."

He shook his head. "I left. I'm no longer a part of the pack," he snapped, releasing me. As he did, a coldness swept over me.

"Lars has threatened to take over, and the pack is frightened. They need you. *We* need you," she said, her eyes pleading. "And although you don't think you are, you'll always be a part of the pack."

"How did you find me?" he asked, his tone guarded.

"You're an alpha, Rylan. We're all connected."

He exhaled loudly. "Where is Lars?"

"Last we heard, he was in Gunnison, probably heading this way."

Rylan cursed under his breath, his hands raking through his hair. "And where's the pack?"

"They're in Montrose, a little over an hour away." Rylan was clearly disturbed. "I'm sorry," she said, looking between us. "I had to come. The pack needs a leader, and if Lars finds them, you know what he's capable of doing. There are only six of us left."

Rylan cursed again. "I'll think about it," he finally exhaled, looking up at her.

"How is your mother?" Keira asked.

He gave her a pained look that made my heart ache. "She's dead."

"What?" Keira's eyes shut tight, and a tiny tear trickled down her frail cheek. "I'm so sorry," she whispered. She stepped closer and handed him a piece of paper. "We'll be here until tomorrow night." Rylan took the paper and shoved it in his pocket.

The entire atmosphere had changed as we watched the girl, Keira, walk away. My heart was breaking for her, understanding what she was going through, but it wasn't my place to say anything.

"What was that all about?" Camden asked, stepping toward Rylan.

"Pack issues," Rylan exhaled. "I'll deal with it later."

"We'll talk later," Cam said and walked away. He also knew it was better not to interfere right now.

Rylan walked back to me and laced his fingers through mine.

"Are you okay?" I asked, gazing deep into his hazel eyes.

But I knew he wasn't okay. I could read his body language and see stress clearly etched on his face. Keira's news had greatly affected him.

But Rylan was strong, a survivor. I had learned he didn't like to wear his emotions on his sleeve, and didn't like to involve anyone else in his problems. He was the type who handled issues his own way. And after hearing what kind of person Lars was, I had a feeling Rylan would avoid bringing his pack into Havenwood Falls. He wouldn't want to risk the safety of my family, or me, and what he was still building here. If anything, he would keep the issue outside of town until it was resolved. And that's what scared me most.

"Hey, you," he said, kissing the tip of my nose. His signature grin was instantly back, putting a smile on my face. "Don't worry about me, cupcake. It's nothing I can't handle."

"I know," I sighed, taking his other hand. I wanted him to know that we were here for him, like he was for us . . . for me. And we would fight for him, no matter what. "We're all here for you. You know that, right?"

His eyes went distant for a moment. I wrapped my arms around his waist and he hugged me closer to his chest. His wonderful scent wrapped around me, instantly calming my nerves.

"I know," he breathed, pressing his lips to my forehead. "I know."

We stood in silence, holding each other tight, watching the last of the glimmering lanterns sail into the endless sky above, until they faded from view.

There were so many new and unanswered questions floating around us. But I still believed in fate and held tightly to it, believing it brought us to this town for a reason.

What did the future hold for us? I didn't know. But like my dad always said:

We'll get through it together . . . like we always have.

WE HOPE you enjoyed this story in the Havenwood Falls High series of novellas featuring a variety of supernatural creatures. The series is a collaborative effort by multiple authors. Read on for an excerpt of *Fata Morgana* by E.J. Fechenda.

HAVENWOOD FALLS BOOKS by Cameo Renae:

Bound by Shadows
Shadows & Spells

OTHER BOOKS you might enjoy in the Young Adult Havenwood Falls High series:

Written in the Stars by Kallie Ross
Somewhere Within by Amy Hale
Cast in Moonlight by Ali Winters
Predestined by Valia Lind

Stay up to date at www.HavenwoodFalls.com

ACKNOWLEDGMENTS

First, I'd like to thank Kristie Cook who invited me to be a part of this amazing world. It's been such an honor and privilege to write alongside all the other outstanding Havenwood Falls authors.

I'd also like to thank the readers. It's because of you that our stories come to life. We appreciate you.

ABOUT THE AUTHOR

USA Today bestselling author Cameo Renae was born in San Francisco, raised in Maui, Hawaii, and now resides with her husband and children in Alaska.

She's a daydreamer and a caffeine and peppermint addict, who loves to laugh and loves to read to escape reality.

One of her greatest joys is creating fantasy worlds filled with adventure and romance and sharing it with others.

One day she hopes to find her own magic wardrobe and ride away on a magical unicorn. Until then . . . she'll keep writing.

HAVENWOOD

FALLS HIGH

Fata
Morgana

E.J. FECHENDA

~ A Havenwood Falls Young Adult Novel ~

Fata Morgana (A Havenwood Falls High Novel) by E.J. Fechenda

Love stinks. Love bites. Love hurts.

Paisley Underwood sings along with the countless songs about love gone wrong, but she's never experienced it for herself. With school, work, and volunteering, she doesn't have time for it. Not to mention, she's a fae on the cusp of awakening, facing unknown changes as her dominant ability emerges. When she starts her senior year at Havenwood Falls High, she has plans to make as many memories as possible with her friends. Falling in love isn't part of them.

A quiet and broody artist, Cole Silver has never been on Paisley's radar except as competition in art class. Also a fae, he went through his awakening over the summer, emerging with abilities he considers a curse. Blending in with humans had been challenging enough before, and now he's a magnet for human women. But he's inexplicably drawn to Paisley, who's thankfully not human.

When Paisley drops everything to focus all of her time and energy on Cole, her friends and family grow increasingly concerned about their unhealthy relationship. Then they discover dark secrets about Cole, his family, and his abilities, and concern morphs into a fight for Paisley's life.

Love stinks. Love bites. Love hurts. Love can be a lie.

FATA MORGANA

AN EXCERPT

COLE

One second made the difference between life and death. Had I been paying closer attention, I could have avoided disaster. Gwen, the owner of Tragic Ink, where I had been hanging out as an apprentice, had finally let me do my own ink, and I was distracted as I left the studio, watching how the natural light played off of the deep blues on my new tattoo. When I stepped onto the sidewalk, I didn't see the human girl coming at me, and we collided. She practically bounced off of me. Reflexes kicked in, and without thinking, I reached out to steady her. The moment my hands touched her bare upper arms, I realized my mistake. I quickly pulled away, but it was too late. The girl's pupils dilated, and her dreamy gaze fixated on me. She was hooked that quickly and already doomed.

Just one touch from me was like being marked by a reaper.

"Hi," she said breathlessly, tucking a stray blond hair behind her ear as she batted her eyelashes. "I'm Emily."

She took a step closer to me, and I took a step back, hoping to keep some distance between us, but the girl eyed me like she was a lioness and I was her prey. The same look I'd seen in another girl's eyes in Colorado Springs earlier this summer. A girl I'd kissed and was now dead. Emily licked her lips and grabbed my hand, not knowing she was already an addict, desperate for her next fix.

Here we were in the middle of town on a warm summer evening, where there were too many witnesses.

How quickly the excitement over doing my own tattoo faded. It had taken me close to three hours as I methodically and painstakingly applied the needle to my pale skin. There was a large probability of error doing work on myself, and I hadn't wanted to screw up. The end result was exactly how I envisioned it—the beginning of a much bigger design that would eventually be a full sleeve.

Even Gwen was impressed and told me I did a good job. Since she barely interacted with me except to tell me when something needed to be cleaned, or to send me on a coffee run to Broastful Brew, I knew that was something. I wanted to be a tattoo artist and own a studio someday, and this experience just bolstered my dream, especially after the nightmare my summer had been so far. And that nightmare was far from over.

I hated what I had become after my awakening, and I was still trying to learn to control my abilities. Of course, I would be the one to inherit a long-dormant gene, passed down through generations. Gancanagh were a rare species of Greater Fae, but there was nothing great about being a gancanagh. It was a curse. My looks were transformed, making me irresistible to human women, but a single touch from me meant certain death. When they came in contact with my skin, the toxin I secreted was more addictive than the most potent heroin and crack combined. And more deadly.

"What's your name?" Emily asked, breaking the thoughts bouncing around in my head. I realized she still had a hold of my hand. Her cheeks were flushed, her blue eyes bright with lust, and she literally buzzed as my toxin coursed through her veins. How was I going to explain to my parents that it had happened again, but this time in Havenwood Falls—our home?

"Listen, I'm sorry for running into you, but I gotta go." Like a coward, I planned on bolting.

I didn't recognize this girl and wondered if she was one of the many tourists visiting Havenwood Falls. Would she be gone before the symptoms kicked in, completely unaware that her time on earth was drawing to an end? I started to extract my hand from her grip, but she stepped forward again, pressing her body against mine. That's when her energy hit me, and my body started to hum from the infusion. I could drain her dry, right here on the sidewalk, and leave her a weak shell until she wasted away, but that was cruel. That was the mindset of a monster—not me.

She was younger than me, but only by a year or two, making her sixteen or seventeen. I was sure I would have known her if she lived here. Emily's other hand slipped into the back pocket of my jeans, and she tugged me closer. She tilted her head up to look at me. Her eyes were dark, completely dilated. Her cheeks were flushed like she was running a fever. Her mouth parted, and she licked her lips. At this point, the roles reversed, and I found her irresistible. Energy, her very life essence, poured off of her, and the need to absorb it took over. Any resistance, any efforts to control myself were lost, and I was weakened by the temptation. Leaning down, I captured her lips with mine, sealing her fate.

PAISLEY

My friends and I stopped our giggling the moment my bedroom door creaked open. I fully expected my brother, Dalton, to be there, ready to shoot us with his Nerf gun again, but my mom's face appeared instead.

"Hi, girls, I'm going to make some cookies and will bring them up when they're done."

This was received with a couple of excited squeals.

"Thanks!" my cousin Julianna called out.

The moment the door closed, the giggling continued. We were talking about boys and who we were excited to see when school started in two weeks.

"He's only going to be a junior, but Will Kasun is fine. Oh, and

Logan is huge. He could bench press me any day," Makenna, my best friend, said. Her cheeks turned bright red before she buried her face in a pillow. She was a cheerleader and spent most of her time stalking from afar during cheer practice.

"Yeah, but Logan is so in love with Serena. She just doesn't see it," Zal said, and Julianna murmured in agreement, unusually quiet and not contributing to the conversation.

"What about you, Paisley? Who are you looking forward to seeing?" Zal asked, breaking the silence and steering the conversation back to a lighter topic.

I tilted my head slightly as I thought about my answer. No particular guy came to mind. "I don't know. Honestly, between work, volunteering at the medical center, and getting everything together for the pageant, I haven't had time to think about anything else."

"Oh, the pageant! Who do you think will be Miss Teen Havenwood Falls this year—do you think you'll win?" Makenna was easily distracted and seized on the new topic like a cat pouncing on a red laser dot.

"I don't care if I win. My mom and Willow basically forced me to enter because it's family tradition." I met Julianna's gaze from across the room. It was like staring into my own, as we had the same shade of violet eyes.

While I had been the one to convince Julianna to enter the pageant with me, I knew she would win. I mean, she excelled in everything. She smiled at me before turning her attention to Zal, her best friend. Physically, those two were polar opposites. Like me, Julianna had fair, almost luminescent skin and where I had purple highlights, Julianna's hair was naturally lavender. Zaltana had dark skin and hair as black as ink. She was the granddaughter of the chief of local band of the Ute tribe, and she looked every bit Native American royalty.

Talking about the coming school year and the pageant made me feel suddenly anxious, and with a dramatic sigh, I fell back against a pile of pillows stacked against my headboard. As if I didn't have enough to worry about between figuring out what to do after high school and the uncertainty of when I was going to go through my awakening, the pageant was an annoyance I could do without.

I was turning eighteen in May, less than a year away, and knew my awakening could happen at any time. Makenna and Julianna, who were both fae, had already gone through theirs. Makenna had to take a week off of school until she learned how to control her abilities. My cousin Willow told me that when she went through her awakening, her emotions were off the chart, like PMS on meth. She'd told me her story a million times, but it never grew old. It was part of Havenwood Falls history. Willow didn't know at the time that she was coming into her full powers as an empath, and had she known what was going on, she might have been able to prevent the Vampire Massacre of 2005.

I tuned out my friends as the conversation returned to boys. All summer, I'd been obsessed with wondering what my dominant ability would be once I went through my awakening. Would I be a bomb-ass gardener like my mom, who could make any plant grow in the most extreme conditions? Would I inherit my dad's healing abilities, which made him one of the more popular doctors at the medical center? Maybe I'd be an empath like my cousin Willow? Who knew what fate had in store for me? I couldn't wait to find out, but was nervous, too. This year was going to bring a lot of change.

I looked around the room at my friends, who were sitting in a circle on the floor in the middle of my room. Taylor had brought a Ouija board and was setting it up. She was the only one out of this group who attended the Sun and Moon Academy. Makenna, with her red hair that reminded me so much of Aster, my former manager at Coffee Haven, grinned at me when my gaze landed on her.

"Get your butt down here, Underwood," she said and patted the empty space next to her. "We're going to conjure up some spirits. Maybe we can call up a smoking hot ghost. Has anyone dated a ghost?"

I eyed the Ouija board uneasily because, knowing Taylor's power, we were going to be bringing a spirit forth. At least she was a competent medium, and I knew she'd be able to send them back. We didn't Ouija irresponsibly. Taylor was a member of the Luna Coven, and they would come down on her hard if she misused her magic.

Later that night, with our bellies full of cookies and milk, we lay down, getting comfortable. I yawned and turned onto my back, staring at the ceiling. I had strung tiny white lights up all around the room, where the walls and ceiling met. These, combined with the silvery, watery light that spilled in from the moon outside, cast my room in a soft, dreamy glow. The house was quiet. Dalton had given up trying to scare us, and my parents had gone to bed. Makenna sighed and rolled toward me. We were sharing my bed while Julianna, Zal, and Taylor were stretched out on the floor with yoga mats and sleeping bags.

"Can you believe we're going to be seniors?" she asked.

"Technically we already are, but I know what you mean. It seems like yesterday we were starting middle school."

"Do you guys remember how nervous we were about being freshmen?" Taylor asked. "I like seriously almost threw up in the bushes by the front steps of the Academy. The seniors then seemed so mature, ya know?"

"It went by so fast. Let's make this the best year ever. Promise?" I said, rolling to face Makenna. "Who knows where we're all going to be this time next year."

Makenna reached for my hand, and we linked pinkies. We had been making pinky swears since we were seven, taking them as seriously as any vow or oath.

After everyone else fell asleep, I lay awake listening to their soft breathing. *How many more sleepovers are we going to have?* We all had decisions to make about our future. Some of us were going to leave Havenwood Falls and never come back, our childhood memories wiped away. Some of us would stay, but adulthood would mold us into different people. We'd be burdened with more responsibility. I linked my pinky with Makenna's again, and she mumbled in her sleep, but didn't wake. I wished we could stay like this forever, that my room could become an impenetrable bubble keeping my friends and me safe from outside forces. With that final thought, I finally drifted off to sleep, blissfully unaware of how quickly things were going to change.

www.ingramcontent.com/pod-product-compliance
Lightning Source LLC
Chambersburg PA
CBHW052004170626
46808CB00007B/2775